HIND POCKET BOOKS

Cows Don't Give Milk

Dr. Promod Batra (1936-2016) was born on 15 October 1936 in Sargodha a city in the Punjab Province located in modern day Pakistan. He was the eldest of five children and his father was an officer with the railways. As a child he was not exceptionally meritorious academically, but was blessed with the talent to learning on his own, think and find simple answers to questions on life. A habit which became his passion and then gave birth to his company – Think Inc.

Cows Don't Give Milk*

*It has to be extracted drop by drop

PROMOD BATRA

HIND POCKET BOOKS
An imprint of Penguin Random House

HIND POCKET BOOKS

USA | Canada | UK | Ireland | Australia
New Zealand | India | South Africa | China | Singapore

Hind Pocket Books is part of the Penguin Random House group of companies whose addresses can be found at www.hindpocketbooks.com

Published by Hind Pocket Books Pvt. Ltd
4th Floor, Capital Tower 1, MG Road,
Gurugram 122 002, Haryana, India

Penguin Random House India

First published in Hind Pocket Books by Penguin Random House India 2019
This edition Published in 2022

10 9 8 7 6 5 4 3 2

ISBN 9789353494193

Printed at Repro India Limited

www.penguin.co.in

FSC www.fsc.org MIX Paper from responsible sources FSC® C047271

CONTENTS

PREFACE

Cows Do Not Give Milk.
It has to be extracted, drop by drop!

Similarly, success and satisfaction in life have to be extracted by manufacturing positive attitudes in our mind, our thoughts' factory.

I was born in October, 1936, in Sargodah, now in Pakistan, in my grandfather's house. My father was posted in the Railways at Lahore. My mother was a very worried young lady, as being the first born among five brothers and sisters, my head was very heavy over a fragile body. In fact, many relatives and friends said to her that there may be a lot of water in my head! My maternal grandfather used to tell my mother, "Shanti, if your son even manages his matriculation, you should be very happy!"

Throughout my life I have been very happy. I did far better than what was expected of me. I did an MBA from the University of Minnesota, USA and authored over 50 management books selling 6,00,000 copies.

During the 1930's, my very anxious mother used to think of several ways to make me good enough in comparison to my cousins. One thing which she did religiously was to give me only cow's milk and plenty of it. She had heard that buffalo's milk makes boys dull! So cow's milk became very important in my formative years.

On August 6, 1947, my father, who was in the Railways, got transferred to Ferozepur where we were given a small bungalow in the Loco Shed area. When Partition took place, three of my uncles and their families came to live temporarily with us. To feed all of us my father got two cows and a milkman to milk the cows. I was eleven years old at the time and was always fascinated seeing the milkman doing such a fantastic job. For reasons more known to me now, my mother used to encourage me to see the process and once in a while, the milkman would encourage me to taste the milk directly — by directing the stream of milk into my mouth. It was a thrilling experience. And once in a while, he would teach me how to milk a cow! It looked so easy when he did it — like walking, but when I started milking the cow, I realised it was quite difficult.

Sometimes only a few drops of milk would come out. I would try for a few minutes and it would hurt my fingers all day. In fact, even now, when I visualize the scene, the pain returns to my fingers!!

Decades passed, seemingly slowly, and one day I saw my younger daughter's 3rd standard book in which there was an article on the cow. And the opening line was, "Cows give us milk..." I was 44. And suddenly, an old thought came to me: *Cows Do Not Give Milk, It Has To Be Extracted, Drop by Drop!*

By this time I had experienced more than half of my life and looking back I realized, yes, life is not so easy! And, yes, cows don't give milk — it has to be extracted and it is a very, very difficult task.

The more I thought about it, the wiser I became. Life

is not simple at all. We need to develop our own mantras to live life fully — extracting success and happiness.

I was a poor student throughout my career. In fact, I failed in class nine and my younger brother was also in the same class! The way my father responded by KFP *(Ki Farak Painda)* made me more wiser. It helped me to face failures. You may like to read the chapter on KFP Vs. BFP *(Bahut Farak Painda)*!!

I could not get a job after my B.Com from Shri Ram College of Commerce, New Delhi but somehow I managed to go to America. My father gave me Rs. 8000, amounting to one year of his pay. In the U.S., my first years were full of challenges and Dale Carnegie's book, *How to Stop Worrying and Start Living,* helped me make those five years the most challenging and the best learning years I ever had. I started as the proverbial dish-washer! I ended up writing, self-publishing and selling my own books because no one wanted to distribute my books.

I was greatly influenced by a statement of Frank Sinatra's. A reporter asked him: "How come you sing so well and you are so successful, and have never got any formal training in music?" He said, "Well, I came from an ordinary family and to earn my pocket money, I used to sing in ordinary bars. People liked the way I sang. My singing was so simple that those who listened to me, thought, boy I can also sing that way!"

This thought influenced me throughout my 33 years with Escorts I learnt simple things like "Learn by listening; understand by reflecting." In fact, I got this poster in Singapore which I liked very much and implemented its meaning to the fullest in my life.

I was fortunate to be in the department of Dealer Development in Escorts. Mr. H.P. Nanda had started his life as a tractor dealer and he well understood the significance of dealers. He, along with my bosses, Madan Agarwal and S.D.S. Mongia, encouraged me to share my management ideas with the dealers and their families. This job was so custom built for my aptitude that I would have given my right eye for it! Maybe, that is why I lost my right eye due to glaucoma.

In Escorts, they never gave me a selling position except for three years as Regional Manager in Bhopal. I did not go into a 'sulk' but I started doing my job very well. I used to work almost four extra hours everyday — reading, thinking, discussing and writing for our dealers. Our dealerships were family businesses. I got involved in that too, resulting in family management books.

In this book you will find simple management mantras, useful both at home and at work. You will find my acquired wisdom in the form of gurumantras which I have been polishing and fine-tuning to almost near perfection. If you take the ideas and add to them your own ideas, you are likely to get a product which will bring you and your family more success and happiness at home and at your work place.

With my very best wishes,

Promod Batra

If you can fill the unforgiving minute, with sixty seconds worth of distance run, yours is the earth and everything that's in it. And, which is more, you'll be a man, my son!

Sukhiram versus Dukhiram 1

A man is not finished when he is defeated. He is finished when he quits.

There are always two ways of looking at life, or at anything in life. A glass of water is either half empty or half full, depending on what you choose to see in it. Some may be lucky to have the grass beneath their feet; while some others may fret and fume and look at the neighbours and envy the green of the grass on the other side. These are attitudes of the mind but those who have the determination to succeed may count on their blessings, one by one, and then resolve to always surge ahead, to chase the frontiers of success.

Even the growing child knows by instinct that he has to hold on to something to begin to walk. So if you feel nervous as hell about tomorrow, look at the horizon and its vast expanse, get absorbed by the feeling of infinity and believe in yourself. Say to yourself again and again: "There is no one who can do it better than me." And then resolve to do it. Take hold of the opportunities in your life and make a success of them. Feel important everyday, love yourself and explore your inner being. And you are already at a stage that few can achieve, bogged down as they are with petty, irrelevant matters.

But what is success? Frankly speaking, it is a relative term. To put it broadly, a successful person is one who is satisfied with himself and lives life happily, *responding* to situations or events in a positive manner, not *reacting* in a helpless manner. And when he dies he leaves behind him an example of a life for others to follow. It is the person who counts all his assets, by way of education, family, friends, material wealth and so on, and tries to give himself and those around him a better life — materially and spiritually. How can this be done? There are no two ways about it. It can only be done by industrious, hard work. After achieving the Miss World title, Aishwarya Rai could have lived an anonymous life, but she chose to work and explore her latent talents and today she tops the Bollywood list of successful stars. She achieved this not by her beauty alone — which is god's gift but by constant hard work.

I shall keep reiterating in this book that cows don't give milk, it has to be extracted drop by drop! In reality, there is no paradise waiting for anyone. You have to build your paradise. And even if you happen to be born with a silver spoon in a home where you don't have to strive hard for material goals, you shall still not be called successful till you achieve something entirely on your own, and have added to the wealth that you have inherited.

The successful person is an adept salesman. Whatever you do in life, whether you have a job or you choose to venture out in a business of your own, you have to sell yourself without ever selling your soul. It may be services or some product that you are selling. A typist, a peon, a writer, a doctor, an engineer, a designer — they are all selling something — they are all selling a service related to a skill they have acquired in their life. Once you have ventured out on your own you are a businessman. The better you are at selling your product, the more success you shall achieve.

This book is a guide, laced with practical examples. According to me a businessperson is any person who wants to make a success of his life. So his problems and how he deals with them are everyone's problems. The businessperson's journey will therefore be a recurring theme like a leitmotif in this book. Also, I have underscored the importance of family ties and the home atmosphere as this is where the journey really begins.

Close to 80 per cent of all businesses in the free world are run by families. If you run a family business or want to run one and have the desire to pass it on to family members, you are in good company. Some of the world's most successful businesses are family-run and in India we have some inspiring examples like that of the Tatas, the Birlas and the Ambanis and the smaller but equally significant examples of hundreds of thousands of concerns built by enterprising men and women.

To start with, you need to have some aspirations and goals. Some entrepreneurs aspire to expand into a large concern, some diversify to hedge market fluctuations or to become their own suppliers, and some are satisfied by the way they are, growing gradually, simply being comfortably off. Most employ workers and managers to introduce efficiency and to promote growth.

The businessperson is any person who wants to makes a success of his life.

In other words, howsoever small the concern, almost every family business is run like a miniature corporate house with the owner as the CEO. This means that they face the same challenges but with greater risks because a single person (and his family) would incur a loss instead of being hedged by the cover provided by a public concern. This makes the entrepreneur work harder and leaves less time for the family or for personal matters.

Therefore, a man who puts his heart and soul in starting and running a business to make his family comfortable is unable to spend time with the people for whom he is working so hard. He ends up creating stresses and strains that later grow so big that they get out of hand.

Even with a second-generation businessperson (who has inherited the business from his/her parents), the same problems arise. The children grow up during the businessperson's most active years, either neglected for lack of time or pampered out of guilt. All of us know of such children who race through city streets in their Marutis or Mercedes', getting drunk or drugged, even stealing for a dare although they don't need the money. We say, "*Bade baap ke bigde bache*" and sneer at them or feel genuinely sorry for their ruined lives.

This situation is common and happens all over the world — it is definitely not restricted to India alone. Perhaps the only difference is that in the USA, for instance, more people have woken up to the problem and found solutions so that fewer families are destroyed because of this.

The way out of the mess is difficult but not impossible and after a point, once fully understood and appreciated, it becomes simple and easy. The basic concern in a family business is *people.* And the dynamics that govern it are the relationships between these closely-knit people like father, mother, son, daughter, in-laws, brother, sister and so on. In most families, these relationships can be difficult but in a business family the difficulties can result in disaster.

A business family, more than any other family, actually *depends* on smooth interactions between the family members.

Relationships indeed have become much more complex these days. Changing values, better education, wider exposure, gender equity and the confusions caused by it are some of the factors that are creating the complexities. To maintain a balance between all these factors is not easy. Some people have succeeded while others have not. But all deserve to know how to play the game without quitting, how to come out a winner on all scores.

I hope that what I have learned over the years, running my own business and all the helpful suggestions and points that I have picked up from others will be of help to you.

Keep two things in mind to make a family business successful and a happy transition from one generation to the next. Both are essential, you cannot compromise on either. The first is love — which means respect, trust, hope, support and mutual understanding within the family. The second is a strong faith in God or destiny and our final accountability for all our thoughts and actions. Without the first, we end up with greed, insecurities and quarrels. Without the second, we end up with a hollow and meaningless accumulation of wealth and disrespect for all human values. What I have discovered is that both these characteristics (love and faith) are usually learned and inherited *from the mother.*

Take the case of Sukhiram and Dukhiram. Sukhiram is the positive guy who will find a way out and will never give up, while Dukhiram will wallow in past miseries, repeat mistakes and eventually quit. Do you want to be Sukhiram or Dukhiram? Obviously the former, so let's find out what differentiates one from the other.

Think before you leap

First, take a positive decision to be a happy entrepreneur and bring happiness to your immediate family, friends and those with whom you interact closely. In other words, take a decision that you will succeed. Not just in making a lot of money, but also making yourself and your family truly happy. Now, having done that your next step should be to ask, "How do I achieve this?" Although individual goals and problems will differ, there are some basic goals and problems common to all of us. Once these are taken care of, you will discover the time, energy and wisdom to tackle more specific areas that need your attention.

Let's start with the first generation entrepreneur, which means you. You are one of those people in the world who are able to make something out of nothing. You have embarked on a risky journey, fraught with all kinds of danger with no one around to throw you a lifeline. You are confident of making things work because you still don't know exactly how big the risks ahead really are. Like the bumble bee that is aerodynamically unfit to fly, but flies nevertheless, you are about to rise up and spread your wings.

What you will do in your initial years is struggle to keep afloat in a hostile environment, cut corners, prune, polish, fight and struggle some more. You are at this stage living on a big dream, stuck together with confidence and blind hope. It takes infinite guts and a bit of foolhardiness but these are the basic ingredients of all successful people in the world, in any undertaking. So you have started on the right foot, no matter what your friends, family and associates say. You already have the foundation that makes a winner. You are starting off as Sukhiram.

Embarking on a long, long journey

The first few years when you begin to carve out the structure of your business from available resources, are years of acute creativity, accidental events and helpless decisions. You may be 25 to 30 years old and already have a history. Your education, the values you have learned from your parents or the environment, the technical or other knowledge that you have picked up or learned in an institution and the finances you were able to collect with some or maybe great difficulty — these are your building blocks. You have to quickly put together a foundation for your enterprise with whatever is available around you — men, material and money. In most cases, it is a mixed and haphazard collection that may or may not be adequate or even really worth much.

What does Sukhiram do? He says, "This is what I have and *I have to make it work!*" Dukhiram would quit straight-away in distress.

Practically all early failures are due to the very accidental and incidental methods adopted by novice entrepreneurs. Very quickly, the stress and strains become too much, unless you are a stubborn Sukhiram at heart. Many successful businesses began in exactly this manner and yet remained afloat long enough, continued to grow, prosper and expand despite all the odds. How does this happen?

To begin with, the successful entrepreneur has a singularity of purpose, *a vision that he never loses sight of.* He is like a hero in the movies, like Amitabh Bachchan (or Rambo) who goes out, single-handedly, with his bare arms and raw courage, fights an army of evildoers and comes back a winner. In the meantime he also has the time to woo his lady and win her hand too. Fantasy? Check the story of most successful businesses and you will find a real-life hero who started off with practically nothing to build an empire that became the envy of his peers. Unfortunately, you may also discover that the hero's grandson quickly sets out to destroy the empire the moment he gets his fingers into the ready-made pie. You may also find that the extended family members are busy fighting amongst themselves in the visitor's room outside, while the original hero is in the ICU, suffering from a heart attack caused by the bitterness around him.

To begin with, the successful entrepreneur has a singularity of purpose, *a vision that he never loses sight of.*

You as a new generation entrepreneur will vow that you will not permit such things to happen. But before you make this worthy promise, you must find out what you need to do, right from the start.

You will need to find out what it is that makes a family effective in business, in terms of how the members relate to one another, how they handle authority and how each member pursues development? The first and most important factor is the family culture. Within this culture, which may be inherited (or may be created by the business-owner) you will design your dreams of continuity and the thrust, goals and values of the business. The role of the supportive spouse is central to this.

Your spouse — your partner in everything

While you dream and plan and scheme to throw all that you own plus whatever you can beg or borrow into your dream business, remember the one person who will be sharing the rest of your life with you — your spouse, your equal partner in the bringing up of your children. If you are setting out to build an empire, then your spouse is the queen or king and your children the natural heirs to the throne. Unfortunately, most men do not consider their wives as being an important aspect of their business plans (even those who love their wives dearly) and believe that her role is only to manage the home front. This, in fact, is the first and often the most disastrous mistake businessmen make. On the contrary, businesswomen, who are a modern breed, almost always seek and get their husbands' support.

Your spouse is your greatest champion or benefactor. She is your most natural ally and supporter. By taking her into confidence (even if you believe that she has no interest in business matters), you will not only have a loyal friend to share your views with but may benefit from an 'outsider's point of view. Besides, by keeping your spouse informed, you are serving another vital purpose. It is she who will be grooming your children, in the initial and crucial years, making them understand you and your dream and preparing them for later responsibilities. So, by treating your spouse as your true partner, you will be doing a favour all around.

Your spouse may begin to cultivate an active interest in your work, share your victories and be your solace when the battles take their toll. Instead of being bitter and resentful when you are absent-minded or too busy, your spouse will know exactly what is going on and give you the space you need from time to time. An uninformed or 'ignored' spouse has every right to become resentful.

On the other hand, your spouse may be one of those people who have a natural head for business. In such cases, spouses become active participants, working, helping and advising to make the business grow in the right direction. Either way, your spouse remains your most important partner — for life.

Remember that Sukhiram takes his wife seriously into account, right from the start. Dukhiram ignores her.

Your heirs — the next generation

The next mistake that entrepreneurs make is to forget the children. Even in a situation where the spouse is an ally and is bringing up the children really well, you will do a disfavour to yourself, your children, and *the future of the business* by neglecting your children. They need the support, love and discipline of both parents, to grow well. Check with most broken families where parents are divorced and you will find either sorrow or delinquency brewing, even at a very early age.

Hurting children is not the same as hurting adults, because adults can fight back, children cannot.

If you are not divorced, you will wonder why this should apply to you. Simple! As a businessperson with very little or no time, you become a parent *in absentia* whom the children see only on rare holidays or returning home tired, upset and 'not to be disturbed'. If you do not find the time for your children, your children will not find the time for you when they grow up. No wonder so many children rebel and refuse to have anything to do with the 'family business' when they are older. In their minds, the business has all along been the demanding 'other' that their parent spent all the time on. For all practical purposes you have been living the life of a divorced partner!

Love is shown in so many ways, but first and foremost, by being available. Parents should be their children's best friends. It is true that parents are the ones who love their children the most. It is equally true that they are the ones who hurt them the most. And most often, with the best of intentions. Hurting children is not the same as hurting adults, because adults can fight back, children cannot. If you hurt your wife, she can talk to her parents or friends and find some solace. Where will your children go, whom will they turn to? When parents hurt their children, the children may cry but repress their real hurt and carry it in their hearts for many, many years. The pain refuses to go away.

When you neglect your children at ordinary times, they get into bad behaviour or mischief to draw attention. What they are saying is, "If you can't kiss me, at least kick me!" In other words, they want to connect with you, no matter which way it happens.

Therefore, spending quality time with your children must be accounted for in your time management schedule as an *investment.* It's an investment that will give you the best returns.

Give time for your children the same importance, if not more, than the time you would allocate for your most valued clients.

Sukhiram considers his children his most important assets. He knows that no matter how much wealth he accumulates over a lifetime, it would turn to ashes if his children went astray. He treats his children with respect and genuine concern. He supports and protects them and gives them his unconditional love. He lets them know (like all good fathers) that Dad is and will always be there for them, whatever the future holds.

Spending quality time with your children must be accounted for in your time management schedule as an *investment.* It's an investment that will give you the best returns.

You may have heard of Ved Mehta, the renowned author who was born blind. Ved's father wanted, more than anything else, to give his son a fair chance in life, especially because he was physically challenged. In his autobiography, Ved recounts that he once overheard his father telling his mother, "I'll sell my soul to give my son the best education possible." His father's love and caring motivated Ved to do his best, to excel in life. He took his Ph.D. in English literature from Oxford University and authored several books. Ved's father spent a great deal of time with him, encouraged him in his studies, consulted him in all important family matters and treated his son with respect, as a responsible human being. Ved grew up to be a successful adult because his father was always there for him.

Dukhiram, on the other hand, will never find time for his children. He believes that they should 'understand' his problems and leave him alone. He can't be 'bothered' by silly concerns because he has too many 'important' things to do.

Sukhiram gets it while others don't

Having understood a few of the things that our success-oriented entrepreneur needs, let us list them. He is daring, visionary, hardworking, creative, talented and cares about the immediate family. But there are many bright and caring individuals who start off in their business and nevertheless fail. So there have to be some more qualities that a truly successful businessperson needs so that the business grows and remains viable for succeeding generations. What are these qualities?

1 A long-term vision that is shared with the family and associates.

Very few businesspeople are good at articulating their

dreams and thoughts about their work, other than in business terms. Yet, they do have a dream, mostly a vague one that does not go beyond a few years. Some may have a vision that spans their own active lives, but most simply think on a five or ten year basis. In fact at 30 or 35 you have another three to four decades ahead, at the least, by which time your heirs would have reached *their* most productive age.

It is time, after the first five years of struggle and when your business is just about to establish itself, to dream in the long term. Let your vision encompass your grandchildren, and their grandchildren — to include five generations down the line. It will give you an edge over competitors who cannot think or plan beyond the present.

Without compromising the needs and urgencies of the day, what you will then begin to do is allow for the changes that are sure to come tomorrow. For this, you need to keep an open mind and acquire the ability to sense the winds of imminent change.

It is possible that you have not found the words to tell your heirs of your visions for the future. It is quite likely that you have not related to them the mistakes you made and the valuable lessons you learned along the way. But if you don't do it now, you will have missed the opportunity to record your struggle and your hard won victories. Those who will take on the job of nurturing your business will not know the true story of its beginning or understand its intricacies. This includes all those core people who work with you and for you, because they too have been contributing to make your business grow. By including them in your vision, by sharing your dream and making them partners to it, you will both substantiate it and make it grow.

It does not matter that you really are the kind of individual who *does* better than he *speaks.* All action- oriented people cannot expect to be fine orators or eloquent speakers, but do talk to your family and associates and share your vision with them.

2 The courage of your own conviction, or faith in your dreams.

Let me tell you a story that will explain this clearly. Many years ago, a man came to Mumbai from a village in Andhra Pradesh to give his family a better start in life. He worked diligently all his life, first as a peon and later retired early as a senior clerk from the company he had served all his working life. He had sent his two children to good schools and his son went on to do an MBA from a prestigious institution. But this man, Rajagopal Shetty, had a personal dream. You see, his mother used to make the most delicious dosas in the village of his childhood. And every time he went home, he would dream of making the same dosas and selling them in his adopted city. When he retired, he received a lumpsum of money and decided to make his dream come true.

With the blessings of his old employers, he opened a dosa stall, right at the corner outside his old office building. He put up a hoarding behind his stall advertising the stall. Each time a customer came, he served him with a smile and asked him to try another 'special dosa' or pack some to take home for the family. His business flourished. Soon, people would come from distant places in Mumbai to taste his incredible dosas cooked in real butter, wrapped in a banana leaf, with an authentic coconut chutney. He had to employ people to help him cope with the rush, particularly after office-hours. Within three years, the stall grew and two more stalls had to be put up next to each other. Then, his son Gopi, passed out with a 1st class MBA degree and visited his dad's stall to see the business. Gopi was shocked. He saw his father's employees putting huge dollops of expensive Amul butter on each dosa. He saw the expensive banana leaves being used once and chucked away in the trash. He saw one employee simply 'hanging around' smiling at customers and helping them get their orders while they sat in their cars, and so on. That night, he told his father in no uncertain terms what he thought was wrong about the business. This was a time of economic recession in the country, the stock markets were crashing and the rupee value (against the dollar) was at an all time low. He told his father (who was ignorant about stock markets and dollar parity and things like that), that he must economise. "Stop using Amul butter Dad, do you know how expensive it is? And why on earth do you need so many helpers? Why should you have to deliver the dosas to people who are sitting right there in their cars? And there's no need to get new hoardings, you don't need them at all."

Rajagopal respected education and his son was an MBA 1st class, no less, so he did exactly what his son told him. Gopi got a job with a company that posted him to Pune. After one year, when he returned, he waited eagerly for his dad to return home at night to tell him how well his advice had worked. Rajagopal came home quite early, looking weary and much older. "You were right son, he said, "there is indeed a recession, my business is crashing exactly like the stock market."

What Rajagopal had as a successful businessman was a sound knowledge about his market, an excellent product and a belief in strict quality control. He also worked on the basis of giving his customers value-added service, and he understood the importance of advertising. But what he did not have was the courage of his own conviction, a faith in himself and in the correctness of his dream. He chose to take the advice of his 'educated' son who only knew theories and had never worked in the marketplace.

3 A firm faith in the future and the ability to accept and be prepared for change.

Most family businesses start off as one-man shows. The owner is the 'management'. He may even be the principal 'product' if the business is in the services sector. Almost invariably, without the owner, there is no business. He picks advisors, if any, selects the employees and it is his shoes that will have to fit the successors. However, the entrepreneur who is creating something with his heart, soul and physical labour is actually building *the foundation* of something much larger because it will grow in the future. Your business is your

No one can predict the future, but we can be prepared for most eventualities. Being prepared and accepting change cheerfully are attitudes that we need to develop no matter what line of work we are engaged in.

successor's legacy, *amanat,* just as you nurture your daughter and help her to grow into a beautiful lady — only to give her away to another man and another family. You nurture your business to give it away eventually to your children and their children.

Your vision of the future will shape the present. If you are prepared for the changes that will inevitably come, you will always be a step ahead and ready for it at most times. No one can predict the future, but we can be prepared for most eventualities. Being prepared and accepting change cheerfully are attitudes that we need to develop no matter what line of work we are engaged in. For a business owner, these attitudes are the keys to the survival of the business.

Success stories are made by men and women who have grit, determination and desire to make a success of their lives.

2 The High Road to Success

Agony and ecstasy in the early years

The early days of a new business, when the entrepreneur is starting out, are lived on a wing and a prayer. It is more of a dream than a business. The motivation that thrusts a businessperson into this danger-zone is the primal urge to do something creative, something that is his 'own'. Most people suffer these pangs and actually start something but a majority give up and get a job because the risks are too great. The few brave ones that do stick on, succeed, but pay a very stiff price.

To start with, the founder of a business has to learn how to play three distinct roles. First, the businessperson has to be a tough, manipulative individual with his suppliers (because practically all businesses start off with less capital than is actually needed), stalling payments to the last and final insult and sometimes one more day. Second, he has to be hard and unforgiving to get total obedience and some sharp practices from the employees. Third, he must be charming and bend over backwards to please the clients because for the businessperson, the client is an avatar of Goddess Lakshmi.

None of the above, however, makes the businessperson mean or bad. On the contrary, the laws of entrepreneurship demand that the entrepreneur be a tough, manipulative, shrewd, demanding and charming person to succeed. This is no place for jelly-livered men or women. And let us say the would-be entrepreneur is basically a dreamer with a product to sell, so becoming a hard-nosed entrepreneur will require change in attitudes to people and life dramatically. The journey is tough. The risks are high, as are the costs, but all of it is compensated of course in the end by the sweet smell of success, if you can just hang in there.

Racing towards success

New businesses require a pace of continuous 100-meter Olympic dashes. There is no time for anything except finding money and off-loading stocks or services. In between, there is the whole business of keeping body and soul together, not just of the family but also of the employees. This is a great pity. If the entrepreneur took *some* time out to *learn,* at least what to expect and how to deal with things by cultivating the right attitudes, he would reduce the price that is paid for silly mistakes.

It is a lot like a love marriage. Two people with stars in their eyes see their own reflections in each other and the initial honeymoon days are so romantic that they never actually stop to think of the hard future ahead.

Contrary to popular beliefs, new businesses are not generally started by people who know what they are doing, *but by people who have something to make or sell.*

It is a lot like a love marriage. Two people with

stars in their eyes see their own reflections in each other and the initial honeymoon days are so romantic that they never actually stop to think of the hard future ahead. They never ask themselves if *this* is the person with whom they will share their entire lives. The deed is done and there is no time to think about the harsher facts of life. After a few months when reality strikes, both will try very hard (if it is in their temperament to do so) and make adjustments. The marriage would, if both made a serious effort, succeed. However, in many cases, rifts develop slowly and the couple begins to wonder what they saw in each other in the first place. So many compromises, so many adjustments, so much hard work would be daunting for the weak and untutored and the only people who would gain something would be divorce and settlement lawyers.

Success stories are made by men and women with grit and determination and a genuine desire to make a success of their lives and who refuse to give up. They take great pains to get solid advice from the right people and sources. They make it a point to follow the advice whatever it costs, because nothing good comes easily. The best things in life are either free or very expensive, they are never cheap!

An avalanche of problems

There are few greater risks in life than starting a new business. After all, there may be very little securities and even little assets to fall back upon.

As a new businessperson, you may have started by borrowing money, either from a bank, or, and usually, additional funds from your life savings, your family and friends, selling whatever will fetch you money. In fact, when you set up a new business, you start off as a pauper. You then begin to manufacture goods or create services, you hire people (whom you also have to pay), you pay overhead costs, you pay for raw material, you pay to keep your home together, you pay and pay and pay. You are paying bills at this stage without a single rupee earned. What can be more risky?

Then, you have to cajole clients to buy your goods or services! And unless what you are selling is in the high- demand short-supply category, you have an even tougher assignment on hand. Add to that the headache of finding the right people to assist you in your dream venture. Employees give up and go elsewhere so that you are constantly short-handed or short-changed. You find that you are the only one working 20 hours a day while those people you pay (from money borrowed on interest) are goofing off or constantly need your presence or monitoring and time, something you simply do not have and cannot afford to give.

Even some tough people give up at this stage and call quits. But you have stuck on because you are fighting the primal battle for survival. Your own survival! And the only equity that you can put in is 'sweat.'

If capital is frozen labour, then sweat equity is frozen guts. Sweat, to the founder entrepreneur, means keeping ahead of the avalanche of problems that are bound to occur. It means kicking dust in the eyes of those who are hell-bent on creating hurdles. The entrepreneur is like a street fighter at this stage and does not sit in a fancy boardroom to plan 'strategies' with his management employees. He *is* the management and will fight with whatever means that are at hand.

The backbone of a good company

As a new businessperson, you have probably surrounded yourself with people whom you think you can afford because you have so little money to spare. What you end up with then, are *sub-standard* employees because you are paying sub-standard wages. You may even have found advisers, willing to give their advice for free or against services/goods at heavily discounted rates. It all works out marginally well because you don't really notice initially that you end up doing most of the work. Your euphoria and enthusiasm have carried you forward and where, in any case, is the time to pause and ponder?

But, if you have a single loyal employee at the start-up stage, this person is worth more than whatever you pay in wages. The rest are just dead wood you are carrying along with you. You will be amazed to learn that most businesses that fail, do so because of early burn-out. The founder burns out his energy and the employees burn down the business through sheer incompetence. That single loyal employee may be the only saviour at the early stage to salvage things because he will share the load with the founder, keep a strict eye on the other employees and fight to keep the business afloat.

M.S. Oberoi: a daring man

Mohan Singh Oberoi, the man who founded the

world-class Oberoi chain of hotels, is someone every upcoming entrepreneur must read about. His life story is a classic case history of all the things that a founder businessman should (or should not) do to succeed in aces. One of Oberoi's greatest strengths was his choice of initial employees. In fact, if the Oberoi chain is so successful today, you can safely say it is because of its employees. Mohan Singh Oberoi, with his ordinary educational, financial and social background had a few fundamental things very clear in his acutely sharp mind. He never found excuses to stop learning. At every stage of his growth, he realised that the best way to get ahead would be to learn something new. He worked hard because he knew he had to add up hours and days of work (drop by drop) to reach the sum total of success he wanted in life. He had big dreams but he did not have a swollen head and knew that he must learn, learn more if he wanted his dream to become a successful reality.

Mohan Singh was just six months old when his father died. His 18-year-old mother, Bhagwanti, a formidable woman as later events would prove, took her baby and went off to her father's village called Bhaun in western Punjab (now in Pakistan) so she could bring up her son.

Mohan Singh studied in the village school until he was 14 and was then bundled off to Rawalpindi. Through his early years, Bhagwanti took fierce pride in her son and made sure he lacked nothing because she dreamed that he would grow up and become 'somebody'.

At Rawalpindi, Mohan Singh saw his first angrez and his first hotel. Both later played the most important roles in his life.

During one of his vacations, when he came home to Bhaun, he met a boy called Shiv Nath Singh and they became friends. Mohan Singh finished his matriculation and chose to move to a college in Lahore. Here, he met his uncle Sardar Sunder Singh, his father's brother and moved in with him. His uncle owned a flourishing shoe business – the Punjab Boot & Shoe factory and seeing his keen eye for design and ability to manage things, his uncle employed him as a supervisor. Mohan Singh was still a student then and had just passed his Intermediate exams, but he decided to drop out because he was more keen to work full time.

At 18 years of age, Mohan Singh started working full-time as Manager in his uncle's shoe factory. But very soon, fortunately for Oberoi's future destiny, events intervened to move him away and push him to new frontiers. On April 13, 1919, the British caused the tragic Jallianwallah Bagh tragedy and in its aftermath of protest, the shoe factory closed down.

Oberoi returned to Bhaun, jobless, penniless and heartbroken. His mother immediately got him married to a pretty 15-year-old girl. After the festivities were over and reality set in, Oberoi decided to return to Lahore since the factory had opened again. It was at this time that Oberoi decided to shave off his beard, a bold decision (since he belonged to a strict Sikh family) that would once again play a role in moving him towards his real destiny. His uncle threw him out in dismay and Oberoi had to return to his village. In the meantime, his wife had given birth to a baby girl, named Rajrani and soon after he returned to Bhaun, the Bubonic plague descended on the village and the small family escaped from there to save the child. They went to a tiny place called Murree near Simla in the hope that Oberoi would find a job there, in some government service.

Fate intervened again and Oberoi failed in his interview in Simla. While walking despondently on the Mall, he had his first sight of Faletti's Cecil Hotel — a palatial 100-room, nine-storey building with powerful and stylish English men and women moving in and out of its grand entrance.

Perhaps it was then, at the age of 20, unemployed, encumbered with a wife and child, penniless but wearing a neatly pressed suit and shining shoes that the dream took hold of him.

Using his native intelligence and charm, Oberoi managed, with some initial difficulty, to get a job at the Cecil as a lowly clerk at Rs. 50 a month, his main task apparently being to keep track of the hotel's coal supply. Owing entirely to his diligence and his impeccable manners, he was soon promoted to Desk Clerk. One day, a notable guest, Barrister Motilal Nehru asked the young Desk Clerk if someone could type out a document. Oberoi immediately took on the responsibility himself and returned the neatly typed document to Mr. Nehru. *This attitude, of walking that extra mile, was just one of the many that defined Oberoi's character and pushed him to greater heights.*

By now, the young couple had four more children, two boys, named Tilak Raj (Tikki) and Prithvi Raj (Biki), daughters Swaraj and Prem. The children spent a great deal of time with their grandmother Bhagwanti, whose unstinting support to her only son Mohan Singh spilled over to his family.

In 1927, Ernest Clarke (his boss at Cecil's) invited Oberoi to help him run a property in Delhi called the Delhi Club on a year's contract. The venture was successful and Clarke then decided to buy his own hotel when the Carlton in Simla came up for sale. Although half the size of Cecil and nowhere close to its pomp and splendour, Oberoi did not hesitate to follow the man who gave him his first break in business. Besides, the poor conditions of the hotel challenged Oberoi. The two men went up to inspect the prospects and negotiate the price. Clarke did not have the sum needed to make the down payment on the property but Oberoi stepped in and tapped his mother's wealthy associates to borrow the required amount.

Soon, Clarke had to leave the country because his wife wanted to go back to England and Oberoi became the sole in-charge. As events turned out, in a few years, Clarke decided that he had to sell the hotel and once again Oberoi was faced with an opportunity, a risk and a decision that would take him to his destiny. His wife, a partner to his dreams, sold all her jewellery, but it was still short of the required sum so they borrowed money from a relative. Finally, on August 14, 1934, M.S. Oberoi became the sole and exclusive owner of his first hotel, the Clarke's at Simla.

Oberoi, the family man at heart

During all these years, the family of five brothers and

sisters was growing up. Mohan Singh's wife, as we saw earlier, played a vital role in his enterprise and became even more influential in the future. The oldest son, Tikki, however, was already a cause for concern, not so much to his father, because he doted on all his children, but certainly to the women of the household. There was a streak of recklessness in the boy, possibly because his father was too busy most of the time and therefore indulged his every fancy to make up for his absence. Then, Swaraj met and fell in love with Gautam Khanna, a very smart, young man. Mohan Singh immediately spotted the potential in Gautam and took him into the family business. And so, the son-in-law Gautam took charge and carried the Oberoi chain (that now included Calcutta's Grand Hotel) to great heights in the future.

Tikki, the older son, carried on a flamboyant lifestyle and married twice. However, his international connections and genuine goodness, earned an enormous amount of goodwill for the Oberoi Hotel group.

Biki, whose schooling took place at St. Paul's in Darjeeling, was less wild, more contained and eventually took on the reins of the business.

Although Mohan Singh (by now he had become Rai Bahadur Mohan Singh Oberoi) indulged the older son more, he knew that it would be Biki who would carry on the legacy. So, from the very start, Biki was always at hand at deals, meetings and decision-making moments so that his growing years were also learning years in the business he would later inherit.

The Rai Bahadur took great pains to surround himself with men of character and loyalty because he was in business where it was relationships rather than anything else that counted. He had the grace at all times to accept suggestions that would improve his services and was unstinting in his generosity towards those who made meaningful contributions.

He had the foresight to understand that 'professional training' at management level was imperative. He was one of the pioneers of sending talented young men abroad for on-the-job training, which today has become a norm for all successful businesses.

Today, the Oberoi chain of hotels consists of more than thirty world-class properties around the world and is considered a benchmark for excellence in the industry. A young dreamer who started off as an assistant in a shoe factory in a small outpost of Punjab has become a household name because he dared to believe in his dream and his ability to make it come true.

The gender war: the new woman

In India, we have a long history of conflicting attitudes towards women. On the one hand, we 'worship' them as mothers and on the other hand, we have left them behind in our development schemes. On the one hand, we have had a woman Prime Minister but on the other, we also burn our brides. The message that children get is a confusion between respect and disrespect.

Yet, women have proved their mettle as students year after year, they are better and harder at work, excellent managers and administrators, they have patience, generosity of spirit and great resilience. Today, with equal opportunities available to them, women have entered every field of activity and have proved their mettle. The time has come to change our attitudes towards women. Since this book is about relationships within business families, this is an exceptionally important subject.

The first thing we must accept is that men and women are different biologically but they are equal in the eyes of the law, equal in every sphere of human activity. Just as two men are not born with equal capacities for physical labour or mental genius, two women will differ.

By setting a standard in your home, by the way you relate with your mother, sister, wife and daughter — whether you are a man or a woman — you will set an example for others to follow.

It is not men alone that have perpetuated the myth of male supremacy; women have played the game too. Many men still believe that a woman's place is in the home, preferably in the kitchen. Many women prefer to play this role. It is so much easier. But a large number of women today with education and an open mind are exploring the world outside their homes and want to contribute something to it. These women have the education and the opportunities equal to their brothers, better than their fathers and should be encouraged in their goals.

One of these women may be your wife, sister or daughter. Could you strangle her ambitions, would you take the responsibility of killing her spirit? Should you fall back upon prejudice, customs or traditions of a bygone era and keep the women of your family behind a purdah created by you? Even the Taliban did not succeed, despite their guns and their harsh punishments.

The woman who chooses to stay at home and prefers the role of wife and mother is a different matter. The choice is hers and it is indeed a full-time job bringing up children with pleasures, challenges and rewards of its own. But whether a woman is a housewife, a corporate executive, a doctor or pilot, she deserves the same respect, as a human being. It is this basic lack of respect for women that has unleashed such terror on our streets where men can tease, molest and harm them with impunity.

If we teach our children the ethics of respect for life in all its wonderful variety, we will slowly but surely bring about safety and security for our future generations. If we are able to overcome our prejudices against women, we will be paving the way for a better society all round. Educated women can bring up their children better. A working woman is contributing to social progress and economic health. A working mother is taking on a dual challenge and needs help, not our criticism. Strong family networking helps a working woman to overcome the problem of childcare. The day we understand the value of family networking, of the stability of extended or joint families, we will create a stable nation with fewer crimes a lesser evils.

Your wife, the mother of your children, should become your friend and partner. By including her in your sphere of activities, even if she does not actively participate in your business,

> **It is never too late to become a student. With the kind of material available for home study today, your wife should not miss out on the opportunity to widen her mind.**

you will be doing yourself a favour. She will have native intelligence and will give you her own perspective on certain matters even if she has had no formal education. She may not understand or be interested in tax laws, but she understands people and their dynamics, perhaps a great deal better than you do. By keeping her informed, by giving her views due respect, by merely letting her in to your secrets, problems and victories, you will find yourself the best and most loyal ally in the world.

I would suggest that your wife should continue her education because it would help her with the children or even grandchildren. It is never too late to become a student. With the kind of material available for home study today, your wife should not miss out on the opportunity to widen her mind. The same holds true for your daughters and daughters-in-law. Encourage them to study and learn whatever they are interested in and watch them bloom into their potentials as human beings.

Take it easy when it comes to inessential matters. On the contrary, address important issues urgently, especially regarding your children, spouse and your extended family.

3 Making a Difference

Ki Farak Painda versus Bahut Farak Painda

Over the years, one important thing I have learned is aptly summed up in robust Punjabi: *Ki Farak Painda* (KFP) or, what does it matter? This is merely an attitude, of being able to shrug things off, get up from the floor after a fall and get on with life. It is also an attitude of seeing things in their real perspective, of being able to pin priorities on the really important things in life instead of wasting time on inessentials. Instead of getting worked up about things that get resolved on their own, or losing sleep over what cannot be helped, or making a mountain of a molehill, smile, shrug it off with a KFP and get on with pressing matters.

Amazingly, I have found that at least 90 per cent of the so-called problems in life belong to this category. For the other 10-odd per cent, we have another pithy saying in Punjabi: *Bahut Farak Painda* (BFP) or it matters a great deal. These are the issues and events in life that actually have serious consequences or can create situations that may go out of hand. Nip it in the bud, take care of these consequential issues as soon as you notice them because, friends, BFP is what will define the difference between peace and the lack of it in your life.

This book is about relationships and about learning to foster relationships while working to build a successful business. Everyone who knows will admit that the first thing that suffers when a business is being founded is the businessperson's family. If a man is so fortunate as to have an understanding and strong-minded wife, he should thank God for this precious gift. But even a super-woman will sometimes wilt under the pressures of managing her family and home, her husband's temperamental behaviour, constant lack of funds and a complete absence of security. The children will shy away from a father who meets them only on special occasions or is always in a rush to get back to work, or is forever wearing a worried frown on his face.

Growing children need your time (BFP)

It is possible that the person who invented the term 'quality time', vis-à-vis a family situation, was a reformed businessperson. Children do grow up well enough with a single parent, in fact, in some cases, with greater fortitude in their characters. But when both parents are there, children expect and *need* attention from both. In the case of a businessperson's family, paying attention to growing children is as much a part of business as balancing accounts or expansion programmes — in fact, more so. Why? Because these children will tomorrow have to manage the same business. It is imperative to sow the seeds while the time is still ripe. It is important that you observe them and find out which one of them is most likely to take the responsibility of running your business as an adult.

Here is a story of a 72-year-old man, Om Prakash Sharma, who started a business when he was a starry-eyed youngster of 22 years. He was lucky that his wife was a tough lady of the old school who managed to bring up their children — three boys — mostly on her own. Today, the oldest son, Amarjit, is 46 and continues to work in his father's business but more as a cowed down shadow than a man. He had studied engineering so that he could contribute to the business that manufactured engineering products, but through his growing years, he remained in awe of his father who barely noticed him. The second son, Gautam, is 42. He was born when the business was making a lot of money, so to him fell the good fortune of a foreign education and exposure to the outside world. He quickly decided to get into another line altogether and became a hotelier. The youngest son was born literally, with a silver spoon in his mouth, grew up as a spoilt brat and made collecting cars his hobby. Although a very bright young man with a degree in Mass Communication and Photography, he chose these subjects because of the glamour that went with them. He does work for his father, in that he handles the advertising for the business (when he finds the time). Sharma's wife, a gentle but sad lady, has taken to religion in a major way and spends a great deal of time visiting holy places or organising *satsangs* with other ladies for company. She and her husband have absolutely nothing in common.

So what do we have in this situation? A patriarch who has worked very hard to make his business a success, so hard, in fact, that the success itself has become the reason for his shortcomings as a husband and father. Sharma still controls his business and has given no real responsibility to anyone else. One of these days, he will pass away without having groomed a successor to pick up the reins. He is a lonely man because he has no one to share his thoughts with. All his life, he did not once think *Ki Farak Painda* (what difference does it make?) — let me spend some of my precious time with my children — until it became a *Bahut Farak Painda* (it makes a big difference) issue.

Life is like that! Before you know what's happening it hits you like a ton of bricks and then it's too late to do anything about it.

A businessperson needs to ensure certain things as he goes from success to success. The only thing that he cannot spare enough of is his time. And that is the one thing that he has to give his family, before it is too late. Don't forget that a businessperson's children have to learn to manage wealth and live a decent and worthy life *despite* it. It is the hardest thing for a young person to do. Wealth opens so many doors, so in effect, the child has so many more means of escape available from the hard facts of life. Children not born with a silver spoon in the mouth, may take to sporting activities, hard studies or serious hobbies to tackle the tougher or meaner aspects of life, the rich child could take to drugs, dangerous activities or worse. He would do it because he has the means for the easier way out.

Life is like that! Before you know what's happening it hits you like a ton of bricks and then it's too late to do anything about it.

Real life bears out this truth again and again. The rich boy who gets drunk and careless and kills a few innocent people on the way; the rich girl, who takes to drugs or elopes with the driver's son, who has not heard such stories? People hush up these tragic stories but behind the glamour and glitter of wealthy families there are many sad stories. Many children of the rich end up dying young, of excesses or sheer boredom.

It is better to learn from others' mistakes; you don't have time to make them all by yourself. By learning from books or from others' experiences, you give yourself a tremendous advantage, a decisive edge that will help you handle various situations.

It is surprising but true that apart from scientific break-throughs and technological advances, there is very little that is 'new' in life. Most business and family decisions have been made over and over again and a great deal has been written on them. What I have attempted to do in this book is to share the stories and examples from hundreds of books that I have read so that you can benefit from this single collection.

"I am doing it all for you"

> **By learning from books or others' experiences, you give yourself a tremendous advantage, a decisive edge that will help you tions. with situations.**

How many times have you, as a parent said this to your children when they demanded your time? All this is for you, that is why I don't have any time. cope I am doing it all for you." The children, when they grow up not having had your time, will remember you as a shadowy figure that played no role in their life beyond providing an 'unlimited' supply of wealth. Why is it unlimited? Because their father never did explain how the wealth came about, what went into it and how quickly it may disappear unless taken care of *on a daily basis.*

There is a story that will illustrate this very common problem. Raj Kumar Sondhi came to New Delhi after Partition. He was a young man then, barely 22, and had seen all the family wealth disappear in front of his eyes. The enterprising youth started a small business, trading in scrap. He was too proud to take any help and besides, he had just got married and had a wife to support. Starting off was not easy, but Raj Kumar persevered and in a few years his business changed, expanded and grew to be a successful venture. He diversified, went into manufacturing machinery parts, diversified again and was manufacturing tools and the business grew and grew. In the meanwhile, on the home front, his family was glowing too. He had two sons and two daughters. Very soon they were teenagers, each one getting an 'excellent' education at very high cost and none of them knew of any of the heartbreaks or sufferings that went towards buying them the many things that they were surrounded with. The eldest son was sent to college, the prestigious London School of Economics. The eldest daughter was barely 18 when they married her into a wealthy industrial family. When the second son, who planned to study corporate law, was in his second year at St Stephen's and the youngest girl was in her final year in school, Raj Kumar had a paralytic stroke. The right side of his body was paralysed and his speech was impaired. He could not even use his hand to write, even after he was declared well enough to go home. Now what?

In all these years, Raj Kumar had not had the time to share anything with his family except for his income. He was very lucky that his long-suffering wife was a tough lady who kept a strict eye on her children and made sure that they received a sound education, both in school and at home. But, she was not God. She had no idea how her husband made his wealth. She was never made 'a partner' in the secrets of the business. She could not teach her children how to succeed their father. The children barely knew their father because he was so busy. He was a kind and gentle man but *he was never there*.

Now, Raj Kumar was very much at home, but since he could not speak or write and therefore communicate in any manner except with the tears in his eyes, once again he was a father in absentia. The youngest son Kabir, decided to quickly learn about the business thinking that his father's employees would help him. When he went to the office, he found out that not a single employee knew any of the vital aspects of the business. His father had managed it all alone. The employees only did what they were told to do and each one knew only that much that they were told on a day-to-day basis so that they had no long-term vision of the past or the future. For Kabir, this was disaster. His father was the sole signatory to most of the bank accounts with only a small deposit being managed by the accountant for petty expenses. So Kabir did not have access to money to keep the business moving. It took weeks before this was corrected through the bank manager, legal applications and so on. It took months before Kabir began to understand bits and pieces of the jigsaw puzzle of the business and suddenly one day Raj Kumar had a second stroke and he died.

This kind of thing can happen to anyone. Keeping the family informed, making contingency plans and being prepared are all essential aspects of a family-owned business. The responsibility lies with the owner so that the family is not straddled with problems and burdens.

History repeats itself

As your children grow into adults, they will marry, so now besides sons and daughters, you have in-laws too. In many business homes, sons-in-law are 'selected', to expand, diversify or join the family business with a particular talent. Daughters-in-law are chosen to blend in with the family ethos or as in recent cases, are treated equally and join the business, if they are so inclined. All of this is a healthy trend. But, once again, unless the core family has a very strong bond, and the children have grown up with the father's affection and teachings, the sons will rebel having an outsider in the business. The daughters may simply want to keep away from anything to do with their father's work and the poor mother will have to contend with all the internecine wars and politics.

We keep returning frill circle to the same thing. Your family is your most important asset, at the same level as your own sweat and financial equity that went in establishing your successful business. Do yourself a favour and give your family the importance that it deserves now, so that the future can take care of itself. Life keeps throwing googlies at you from the blind side, so the only way to survive is to develop a hindsight. It is worthwhile, at the age of 30, 35 or even 45, to imagine what the next 20, 30 or 40 years will be like. This is like creating a military campaign during peacetime. It is known as 'being prepared', the useful motto of the boy scouts organisation.

Discipline begins at home

How do we prepare for the future? We make plans for regular affairs and hold rain checks for contingencies. For any successful person, the first important step is to give his children, both sons and daughters a sound, competitive education. Through their growing years, while they are students, a large amount of time will be spent in getting this education. Making strict but reasonable rules that the family must follow is a very good way of ensuring a healthy attitude to live. Discipline is an essential factor that must be built into growing children to give them a sense of security as well as teach them not to take anything for granted. Since all their needs are taken care of, children should *never* be given unreasonable amounts of cash to spend, no matter what. They should instead, be taught to have a healthy respect for the hard work that goes into earning money. In western countries, most enlightened families, no matter how rich, insist that their teenaged children actually *earn* their pocket money. In India, this is unfortunately not yet a norm, still, it is never advisable to give children whatever they ask for. This will make them disregard the fact that life is not a bed of roses and that one has to earn a living. Even if it is true that the next five generations do not have to earn a living because you have already amassed so much wealth, let me assure you that no one can forecast what tomorrow holds. One market crash, one earthquake, a war or a single bad decision can destroy everything in a few moments.

The greatest legacy that you can leave your children is to make them worthy, independent human beings that can survive a disaster and start anew.

In-laws or out-laws?

When you find the right girl for your son to marry, or if he brings home his chosen bride, you have a new member in the family who will be a part of it, forever. An intelligent man will immediately treat the newcomer with the respect she deserves as a family member. Unfortunately, in a large number of families, the newcomer is either ignored or treated as an outsider. This *bahu* syndrome is so common that it has become the theme of several popular TV serials. It seems that a great number of people are able to identify with one or the other member of such reel-life families with real-life events. Most daughters-in-law today are educated young ladies with visions and dreams of their own and can contribute to the business family in a sensible way. Even if she chooses to be a full-time housewife, her contribution to her husband's life would be immeasurable. She will be the mother who will bring up the children and heirs of the next generation. Her role is pivotal for the third generation businessmen or women who will inherit your wealth, your grandchildren.

> **Most daughters-in-law today are educated young ladies with visions and dreams of their own and can contribute to the business family in a sensible way.**

The son-in-law who enters the family with a direct relationship to your business, as a financial equal or with an education or talent that can help your business, is a natural ally. But life is never quite that simple. Very often, despite a thorough check-up into the boy's family background, what you land up with is a spoilt fellow, a wastrel or someone with bad habits, the product of busy parents who neglected the son. What do you then do? It is a tough situation. Possibly, the best thing to do is to avoid such an eventuality but if it is *fait accompli,* then the only thing to do is to take on the reforming of such a son-in-law right from the start — by giving him responsibilities that he can manage, by giving him respect (that may not be actually due) so that he is reformed eventually or by pulling up his socks. Since at this stage, he is still a young man, there is the likelihood of his learning something provided he is treated with respect and expected to perform his duties. There are no pat solutions, but it is not an impossible task either.

The benevolent patriarch

In India, the concept of the extended family still flourishes, especially so, in business households. Your sons and daughter-in-law come into this category and very often, a very delicate balance has to be maintained. The first reason is always because your children's peace within their new families become crucial. Your role as a benevolent and caring parent is to make sure that you do not become the cause of a quarrel in your children's new families. Instead, you can play an important role in cementing a bond that is going to last a lifetime.

Sometimes, particularly when your children have chosen their own life partners, you may find it difficult to get along with the father-or mother-in-law. This may be because of their different backgrounds, culture or whatever. Just as a smart businessperson has to deal with a variety of customers, traders and vendors, you should use your inter-personal skills in establishing at least a workable relationship with them — no matter how different or difficult they may be as individuals. This is something that will be entirely to your advantage in the future.

The third generation

You are probably wondering why I am going so far into the future, especially if you are a young person, only recently married. Well, buddy, as I said before, it will do you only good if you think of your future now and plan for it today so that you are prepared in advance. It is true that a lot of changes are going to take place and hopefully, you will remember at all times to factor in these changes and go along with the times as you grow older.

Hopefully you will actually look forward to your grandchildren. I myself have grandchildren and they give me immense pleasure. I teach them and learn from them as well. They are the future generation and each generation gets smarter, one of nature's gifts to ensure the progress of mankind. By the time your grandchildren come along, you should be ready to hand over most of your responsibilities to your heirs so that you can at last relax, enjoy the fruits of your labour in comparative peace and have some fun in the company of your grandchildren.

Unfortunately, a lot of businesspeople can barely recall how many grandchildren they have and even forget their names. These are the people who have spent their lives nurturing their business at the expense of their family's real welfare. These are those people whose success tastes like the ashes of failure when they lie unloved and unhappy on their deathbed. Don't let that happen to you.

The one good thing about life is that we are all given a second chance (and a third and a fourth) if we only know about it and grab it before it is too late. For the businessperson, who has *had to* spend early years, struggling to keep the business afloat and could not give adequate time to the children, the second chance is with the grandchildren. What you are unable to give your own children, you can make up with the grandchildren. In the first place, grandparents have a natural affinity with their grandchildren because of the generation gap. They also have, by then, mellowed, learned from their mistakes, experienced a great deal in life and are not in a constant state of war with life.

By teaching your grandchildren all that you have learned in life, by becoming their mentors, what you end up doing is take on the responsibility of the parents (who are running the business now), without having to sacrifice the time so crucial to the business itself. This is a God-given opportunity to actually perpetuate the business and at the same time perpetuate the family. You, as the experienced founder-businessperson are an invaluable fount of knowledge and your grandchildren will be able to appreciate what went into the foundation of the business.

It is not at all surprising therefore when we see third generation businesspeople taking a family business out of a rut and pushing its frontiers. This happens where the founder gives time to the grandchildren or where the grandchildren *are able to respect* the contributions of the founder even if the founder dies before he can teach his grandchildren anything. What the founder in the latter case leaves behind, is a legacy of goodwill, good memories and a tacit education through his/her examples.

If your trusted family members make a few mistakes, remember, *Ki Farak Painda,* because it is through actions that we make mistakes, and these mistakes teach us to do better next time. If we do nothing, we make no mistakes, but then nothing gets done either.

No dream venture is a day's affair. Sensitivity, intelligence and humility should be your three main assets along the way.

Respond, Don't React | 4

Lighting the long fuse

A person who starts his own venture needs 48 hours in a working day, the fortitude of a saint, the temperament of a street-smart crook, the creative abilities of a Michelangelo and the genius of an Einstein to survive and succeed. In reality, what we find is that the founder-entrepreneur is just an average person with an extraordinary dream and a crazy will to make the dream come true.

In the process of finding the time, managing the finances, making something out of nothing AND attending to the growing demands of family relationships, he will sometimes simply lash out at whosoever is nearest and least expected to react. This is a common reaction to stress. However, whenever you are hit by such impulses, you should pause and think.

Anger or aggression as a reaction to things that are going wrong at work against innocent family members makes no sense at all. What does it say about you? Mainly that you react without thought. This is like a matchstick flaring up at the smallest friction. But you are not a matchstick, you are a thinking, rational and intelligent human being with a consciousness as yet unmatched by any living creature. We, human beings, can 'control' every emotion, we can make something out of nothing, we can rise above our situations and we can visualise and prepare for the future. Instead of reacting in a rush, what we need to do when we get angry, is to think of a long, long fuse. This is an excellent way to control our anger, because as the fuse starts to burn, we have given ourselves the time we need to control ourselves and then *pour some water on the fuse to defuse it.* So instead of an explosion, there is peace.

In our anger, we hurt our children by using harsh words such as, "I'm fed up with you", "Where will you end up at this rate?" "This son of mine is too dumb to be my own flesh and blood!" "Why can't you be like Rahul, (or your sister, or the neighbour's son)?" By using such harsh words, we take away a child's self respect and by doing it often, we actually create an image that the child begins to believe in "I'm dumb!" This is a terrible thing for a child to believe because he will actually become dumb by not bothering to make any effort, since his father or mother has told him that he is dumb.

In our anger, some of us even beat our children although many enlightened parents have understood how much harm this does and control themselves. Imagine that a video camera records you while you thrash your child and then it is displayed on Zee TV or Doordarshan for the world to watch. How would you feel? Most parents when asked this question agree that they would feel extremely ashamed.

The real 'you' is what you are in the dark or behind closed doors. It is very easy to pretend to be a kind, generous, calm, happy, jovial, friendly, honest, caring, truthful, *positive* person in public view. Who you *really are* is known only to very close family members and perhaps the domestic help at home. Most people lead double or multiple lives, showing different faces to different people as the circumstance demands. We all, to some extent at least, wear masks because living in a large society demands this. But your basic character will emerge in your dealings with your family when the doors to the outside world are closed.

> **How do we control our anger? First of all by admitting that anger is ugly, that it is unhealthy and that by reacting in anger, we reveal our own weakness and bed behaviour.**

The real problem, as many parents admit, is that we are not able to control our anger. How do we control our anger? First of all by admitting that anger is ugly, that it is unhealthy and that by reacting in anger, we reveal our own weakness and bad behaviour. The fault lies in us, not our children. We tend to make a lot of excuses, but the fact remains that the anger is created by us and has to be controlled by us. If we have hurt our children or reacted in anger, we must ask for their pardon.

As a founder-entrepreneur, one thing you can take for granted is that many things would go wrong at first. Unless you are so favoured by Lady Luck (which is something not many of us are), that whatever you touch turns to gold and every road you travel is paved so smooth that you glide through without a bump, things would go wrong. In fact, things that go wrong will also teach you how to make them right — a lesson that is learnt without expensive and time-consuming institutional learning.

If you are starting your own business, by the time

you are both rich and successful, you will be in your 50s. You, as a start-up businessperson, cannot be sure that you will succeed but it is some sixth sense that tells you that you will. You should plan both for success and wealth right from the start, because if you don't, then the problems we will discuss here are sure to come up.

All of us know that we collect our karmic rewards as we move along in life. Every act has its consequences for the future, some that we can predict, some that we cannot, some that are known and others that are unknown. Tomorrow's facts are usually the results of today's acts, whether committed, omitted, conscious or unconscious.

These are the lessons that we learn from the Bhagvad Gita. What you do, say and think today will show up, good or bad, tomorrow.

In business, one thing is sure. Each of your initial acts and decisions, such as starting your business alone or with a partner, how much money you put in as equity, how much you borrow, at what cost and From whom, how you hire your employees, choosing, accepting or rejecting opportunities, all of these and more, will eventually decide how successful you become. You will feel the impact of each of these decisions later.

> **Tomorrow's facts are usually the results of today's acts, whether committed, omitted, conscious or unconscious.**

All your choices are consequences you will feel later. When I meet businesspeople who are encountering serious problems, what I most commonly hear is that "this is not what I had planned for." Precisely, because in fact they hadn't planned for that aspect of the business at all! Whether it is to do with a problem related to employees, finances, suppliers or problems at the home front — it is lack of planning that causes the problem in the first place.

The businessperson's accounting system remains inadequate, a maze of confusion designed to fox the Income Tax department but it ends up clouding the management process.

Don't be too secretive

When you start to make a lot of money (probably for the first time in your life), you become superstitious and secretive. You will try your best to keep the real bottomline figures to yourself, afraid to share it with either your employees or your family. As a result, both the family and the employees work in a fog of confusion, cutting corners, unable to create a dynamic decision process and thereby reducing overall efficiency. The businessperson's accounting system remains inadequate, a maze of confusion designed to fox the Income Tax department but it ends up clouding the management process.

In fact, a good accounting system, custom-made for your business, is an excellent management and educational tool. A competent accountant is your best investment in the starting years, a man or woman, who will reveal financial facts selectively, in the right quantity and at the appropriate time. This gives employees a sense of direction, a sense of what needs to be done to cut costs, improve efficiency and also where they can go ahead and invest for a better long-term profit.

If you keep all the good facts to yourself, *you* may

become smarter, but *your employees* will become dumber because they haven't been told how productive their work has been. They may even quit after a while seeing a dim future in your business since all they may have been told so far is that you are not making much profit because you are afraid they will ask for a raise or a bonus.

Let your family share your success

If you share your success with your family, they will learn something about you and also feel proud of you. Your children will feel a sense of pride to join you in your business because they have seen you struggle and come out a winner. They will also feel a sense of responsibility to make your business even more successful by their own inputs.

It is quite possible that some of your family members are already on the board of directors of your business. Perhaps your spouse, a sibling or child are on the board, but are they *working* directors? Most probably not, because if you are a founder-entrepreneur you probably chose to keep all the real decision-making powers to yourself and the board of directors is just on paper to comply with company laws.

What this implies is that you cannot trust anyone to know, understand or carry on your business, even as a working partner while you are around. What will happen, if, God forbid, you suddenly meet with an accident and die? After all, no one is born with a guarantee of life for any given period of time!

If you really care about the future of your business

and your family's welfare, it is absolutely necessary that you build up a second line of defence, a rear-guard that will pick up the gun in case you fall. In every strategic organisation, you will find that proper training is given to create this second-line of managers at every level. These second-line of managers take over the functions of their bosses in an emergency such as an illness and even as a routine when the bosses are on their annual vacations. This is sound planning. I know that you are the founder of your company and you are the one who knows every detail of the business, but don't you think you should start preparing your trusted lieutenants, whether a family member or an employee to take over sometimes at least?

This way you will also begin to understand how well (or badly) those whom you have trained, will manage the business on their own. If you trust your wife, son, brother or even your Munshiji, you will find that you have some additional free time to pay attention to other equally important matters. You will also find that the trust you place in others is returned many times over in loyalty, creativity and an honest effort to make things better for the business.

> **If you really care about the future of your business and your family's welfare, it is absolutely necessary that you build up a second line of defence, a rear-guard that will pick up the gun in case you fall.**

Start training a protégé early

Unlike the human body, the family business is founded

and meant to survive the founder, hopefully for several generations. What this means is that while at any given time, the business is 'headed' by one President or Chairman, two others are being groomed to take over the responsibilities.

Take the example of young Priya Paul who runs the Park Hotel in New Delhi. She was in her early 20s when her father died. He had already started the operations of this five star hotel when he suddenly died. Priya quickly tightened her belt and *responded* to her new situation instead of reacting with grief and frustration. She assumed position as the head of a business she knew little bit about. It was a matter of sheer luck that Priya was such an enterprising young woman with grit and determination to make a success out of the venture.

But all heirs are not like Priya Paul. In fact, most of them, brought up within an environment of wealth and ease, do not pick up the required discipline needed to run a business. They have to be very carefully groomed for it, right from the start.

It must also be acknowledged that as a founder businessperson, you may not be so fortunate as to automatically have one or two children who want to enter your business. They may choose to build careers for themselves, they may be artists or may prefer to teach or to become lawyers or doctors.

Therefore, without imposing your will, you have to plan early and expose your children, to the 'interesting' aspects of your business. Then perhaps, one of them will pay attention and begin to learn the intricacies and mechanisms that make your business work. In effect, instead of *reacting* in anger because your children are not interested, *respond* by showing them how fantastic your business is.

Let me tell you the story about the Goels, a typical, conservative Baniya business family.

Motilal Goel of Mathura founded Motilal Pesticides (India) Pvt. Ltd. after his younger son Shyam Sunder returned with a much-coveted degree in Chemical Engineering from London. The youngest son, Vishnu Prasad, did his B.Sc. in Agriculture but took to the mining industry, making forays into Rajasthan and trading in ores. The eldest son, Manohar Lal, was inducted into the newly founded company and after a few years, Vishnu Prasad also joined hands with the rest of the family.

Here is a typical Baniya family steeped in the age-old customs and traditions of trading and doing business. The one thing that this family appreciated, perhaps more than most typical Baniya families, was education. Each member of the family received a good education—to the extent that the children, all the three brothers, were bundled off to boarding schools because Mathura did not have really good schools. In 1975, the family moved to New Delhi and established their business there, for better opportunities and because they were expanding.

Consider the case of Vikas, Vishnu's son, who was initially sent to Lucknow's Colvin Talukedar College (a good high school) and later to Woodstock in Mussoorie, an international school run by Jesuits and very American in its culture.

Vikas recalls that his father was always travelling and they rarely met, even though his visits to Delhi and home were restricted to summer and winter vacations. "It was my mother who insisted that I went to Woodstock. My cousins were already in that school and doing well. My Dad wasn't so keen, but Mom was determined. She wanted me to get that exposure."

Given the contrast between a traditional home culture and the school's American environment, there was a degree of alienation at first. But Vikas says, "It didn't take very long for me to realise that my own traditions and culture made a lot more sense, at least as far as I was concerned."

While still in school, Vikas was very keen to go into Hotel Management, a popular career choice in the early 1990s. *That was when he first felt his father's forceful influence.* Despite the general lack of communication due to his father's long absences (because his work involved a great deal of travelling), Vikas found that his father had thought a great deal about his future. He refused to agree.

"By the time I finished college and got my B.Com, I was older and more reasonable. I agreed with the family and decided to take my chances here. I was still in college when I started going to Dad's office and soon I had started off creating a new line for myself. Dad did not interfere and let me just hang around and see what was going on and learn things on my own. I realised that it would make good sense to develop our own line in equipment for spraying chemicals, a sort of an offshoot of our basic business. And I went about surveying the market and found that it had an excellent potential. It is now a top-of-the-line division in our company and we are counted as the best in the business among our competitors."

Given the exposure to Woodstock, did it ever occur to Vikas that he might want to choose his own life partner? Apparently not! According to Vikas, the girl chosen by his family was perfect and today the charming young couple are proud parents of two beautiful children.

The business is doing well. Not the best in the country, but among the best and reputed to be the best in the quality of their products. The values cherished by the family are carried into the business, it's there in quality consciousness, in customer satisfaction, in surviving in a competitive field with honesty and hard work.

True to tradition, the new generation, Vikas, is bringing about the changes that our difficult times demand. Instead of simply 'selling' chemicals (pesticides in particular), Vikas is orienting the business to be more market driven, taking customer needs in marketing strategies, packaging and so on into greater consideration. The one area he will not compromise on is quality because that is one thing that the family prides itself on. "In a couple of years I will be taking on more responsibilities. At this time, my Dad has great confidence in me but feels that I still need to learn more."

Motilal Pesticides (India) Pvt. Ltd. is a typical Indian family business. Family members hold all top management posts. That is how they prefer it to be, grooming the next generation, giving them exposure and hands-on experience to carry it forward. Despite his mild American accent, Vikas is Indian to the core and proud of his heritage. Fun loving and modern in his outlook, conservative in his values, highly principled and a happy family man. The best of all worlds!

What Vishnu Prasad did was to *respond* to his son's initial desires to go abroad by giving him an opportunity to check out the family business. He did not *react* with anger but responded with firmness. Because all along, as Vikas agreed, Vishnu Prasad, despite his hectic schedule, had given a lot of thought to his son's future. In return, Vikas responded with responsibility and maturity. He took his chances and joined the business. Given a somewhat free hand, he expanded the business, adding a new division, which he worked very hard to make successful He also responded with maturity when it was time to get married, and agreed with his parents' choice. Both the inlaws get along very well, because they got together by mutual choice and consent.

You have to mould your children to be responsible citizens. Give them a sound education and expose them to good learning. Even at a very early stage give them a little bit of both freedom and responsibility.

5 No One is a Perfect 10

Teach your children how to fish

Having established a successful business with your blood, sweat and tears, you need to plan for the long-term that will do justice to your hard won victory. Your hope is in your children. You have to, whenever you can, get involved in discovering the skills, aptitudes and interests of your children. Your spouse will be a great help in this matter. Your children have the right to seek their own destinies but given the right education, it is likely that at least one of them may choose to continue your business.

There are absolutely no guarantees as to how your children will turn out as adults, but, as a parent and a businessperson there are certain things you need to do, right from the start, to ensure that your business has a fair chance of surviving and remaining in the family.

All your children may not have equal capacities, talents and skills. The first thing that you should do, as a responsible parent, is to ensure that your children have a truly sound education as a foundation for their future. The school you choose for them even of the primary level, is very important. Don't forget that your children will spend the best part of their growing years in this school, inculcating both the good and the bad that the school environment offers. There will be peer pressure, there will be social circles and teaching methods, all of which will determine to a large extent, how your children turn out. Unless the home front is so strong that it overrules some of the attitudes that the school may help to create, you may find that your children have picked up a few habits.

In New Delhi, sadly, some of the better schools where wealthy parents send their children, have unhealthy reputations. This does not mean that all the children who leave these schools have bad habits. It is just that these schools have other children who are 'spoilt' by their parents, permitted to be extravagant and irresponsible and indulge in wasteful activities. If the home environment is secure and loving, with a disciplined but open-to-discussion policy, children do not feel the need to give into peer pressure. So many children are simply influenced by friends to try out things like smoking, drugs and alcohol for instance, because it is the 'in' thing.

A healthy environment at home where children are able to communicate their fears and feelings with the parents or any other adult will nip things in the bud, and prevent catastrophic events later.

> **If the home environment is secure and loving, with a disciplined but open-to-discussion policy, children do not feel the need to give in to peer pressure.**

It is the parents' duty to teach the children how to behave with responsibility. In most cases that I have seen, the rich parent, who has seen struggle believes, "My children should not suffer the way I did. They should get all the things that I did not have as a child.” This is not wrong in itself. We all aspire to give our children the best.

However, by ‘giving’ your children endless supplies of ‘things’, such as the most expensive toys and imported chocolates when they are small and expensive gadgets as they are growing up, fancy cars as soon as they can drive around, huge amounts of cash by way of pocket money, allowing them to stay out late at night (“everyone does it”), what you are doing is *indulging them.* And whom are you indulging? Actually you are indulging yourself, your own desires to “give them what I did not have”. And in the process you are ruining your childrens’ prospects to grow up as responsible adults.

A healthy environment at home where children are able to communicate their fears and feelings with the parents or any other adult will nip things in the bud, and prevent catastrophic events later.

I am sure you recognise what I have just described as the most common problem in business-families. You have seen it all around you, and have read of the disastrous results of this pampering in newspapers when a drunken teenager kills someone due to rash and negligent driving in middle of the night.

Your children are your most valuable assets. Nurture them, guide them and give them all the love that you have. Most importantly, teach them how to be good human beings, so that they can take their rightful place in society and contribute to it.

You have to ‘teach your children how to fish. Let me tell you a story to illustrate this point.

There was a fisherman who started off, like all other fishermen, as an apprentice. He would go along in other people's fishing boats and help, keeping the nets in good order, repairing the boat, pulling in the haul, sorting out the fish and so on. Being a diligent and hard worker, he was soon able to own his own boat and in a few years, a fleet of boats. He became a successful, rich fisherman. His children went to the village school for a while, but since it was much more fun to play in the sand and the sea, they dropped out. There was always so much to eat at home that they had no worries. Then one day, the fisherman had a heart attack and died. The children knew a lot about fish. What they didn't know anything about was how to catch them. So, within no time at all, they lost their father's business and became poor: What the fisherman had failed to do was to teach his children how to fish.

Your life, your wealth and your present security — none of these are bottomless wells your children can dip into forever to get what they want.

Don't let your children believe that money comes from ATM booths or that all the goodies they get are for free. You will be surprised how many children grow up taking their wealth and position in society for granted. When we are young, we rarely, if ever, think of death as something that will happen to us or to our parents. Without making a big fuss, it is necessary for us to teach our children all the lessons of survival that we have learned.

Since it is impossible to have perfect children because no one and nothing is perfect, what we need to do is increase their scores with our own efforts. Start giving them marks mentally. If you are a good mentor, you will have the satisfaction of finding out that your children score an average of 7 or 8 when they grow up. How do you do this?

Expose your children to real life

In a large number of business families, the children are treated with kid gloves, as if they are made of wax and will melt in sunlight. The boys are treated like little *'yuvrajs'* whose every wish is granted immediately (until they learn to believe that they will always get what they want). The girls are treated like budding queens with domestic servants running around them with food, picking up toys and generally mollycoddling them. Walls and barricades are built around these poor children so that they rarely get to know what the real world outside their homes is all about. From air-conditioned homes into air-conditioned cars with tinted windows, visiting equally wealthy air-conditioned homes for parties, these children are shocked out of their wits when faced with the outside world.

Perhaps you have not sheltered your children quite as much. But do they understand that everything is limited? Your life, your wealth and their present security, none of these are bottomless wells they can dip into forever to get what they want.

None of us are perfect, so there is no reason to get worried or upset if you have made a few mistakes so far in bringing up your children. In fact, *there is no perfect formula to bring up perfect children.* What we can do though is try our best. We can learn from our own mistakes and the mistakes other people have made, we can learn from success too. Most of us rely on our intuition when we bring up our children because none of us have been taught parenting formally. Most of us actually follow exactly what our parents did when we were younger, which is why so many families show a strong 'family trait'. In fact, in many cases this method works quite well, except that each generation has to adapt to the changes around them and in keeping with the social development, take decisions on 'new' patterns of behaviour. And usually, this is where mistakes take place, especially in first generation business-families. There are no yardsticks available to make these new choices.

Take, for instance, the basic area of education. You may have had an adequate education, but things have changed dramatically since your time. The opportunities available today, were not available even ten years ago and things are moving so fast that even in education, many things are becoming obsolete. In our times, a BA degree held a lot of value. Today, it is close to meaningless. We had few of the career choices available to our children and had to think in terms of engineering, medicine, law, business management and the administrative services as main-line careers. Our children can opt for a variety of courses that they can pursue directly related to a career or even as an academic. In fact, the options have become so wide that a whole new facet of education, that of 'counselling' students has sprung up, which is itself a career option.

In the area of social skills and behaviour as well, our children are exposed in schools and colleges to a wide range of possibilities. Entertainment has become big business and one of the special targets of entertainment marketing is the child. 'Catch them when they are young' is the market mantra. So what happens when your 15-year-old daughter tells you that all her classmates are going to the disco and that she cannot miss it? Or, you are faced with an 18-year-old son who wants his 'wheels', *now.* Do you give in, do you bail out or do you yell at these kids for being ungrateful wretches? It isn't easy at all. In fact, bringing up children is one of the toughest jobs in the world.

Create happy times

One basic thing you need to do is instill certain discipline and rules for the whole family. Without being too rigid, these rules should apply to all. For instance, the family *must* have at least one meal together. Usually, this turns out to be dinner when everyone is expected to be home at a given time. Make the most of this regular family get-together time. Allow mealtimes to be always pleasant, light-hearted and stress-free. Use the time to catch up with your children's day, so you are aware what is happening in their lives on a daily basis. Very often, we lose track of what our children are up to, until it is either difficult or impossible to change course.

Start off with the belief that your children, like you, are NOT perfect. They will make mistakes, just as you did, and every generation will. Don't make a big issue of a mistake, and never at mealtime. Let every dinner be a memorably gentle time when the children visibly see your kindness, experience your genuine interest in them and feel loved and cared for and secure in their home. What you are doing for them here will cost you nothing but will give them such a tremendous sense of belonging to a good, stable and friendly family that it will see them through a lot of turmoil later.

If this routine is followed faithfully, see the changes it will bring. Firstly, the change will be in you. If you decide to make this mealtime as described above, firstly, the tensed muscles around your neck and back will relax. You are looking forward to a pleasant time when you can forget everything else while you enjoy the presence and the company of your spouse and children. You can share some funny anecdotes with them and listen to theirs. You will find yourself smiling, feeling playful and secure too.

One day, as I was leaving the home of a businessman, I met his ten-year-old son, standing alone, staring at his neighbour's lawn. I stopped to say hello and noticed a man and a boy tumbling around on the lawn next door. The boy looked up at me with sad eyes and confided, "That is Rohit and his dad, they are friends. I see them rolling on the lawn or playing games together everyday. He is in my school and comes first in his class. I don't remember my father hugging me even once."

That sorrow may eventually turn into anger and hostility against his father. Don't let that happen to you!

Freedom and responsibility

The making of your fortune is in your hands, and so is the

building of your spirit. *Freedom* plays a basic and fundamental part in the development of one's spirit, yet few people realise it. Few of us are consciously aware of the freedom we exercise every time we accept or reject an instinct or an idea. The core strength within human beings is the freedom to choose how to respond to life's challenges. We can face a challenge with complaints like Dukhiram's or with an attitude like Sukhiram's: "This is a difficult, distasteful thing, but I have to do it, so I'll do it well." This attitude will make your job easier and will leave you with a sense of accomplishment at the end. In fact, discovering your freedom of choosing your own attitudes towards life's challenges will affect your rate of success and happiness in life enormously.

However, freedom comes with a twin — responsibility. Either one is useless and even harmful without the other. In fact, responsibility is the foundation of human existence just as freedom is its driving force. I have observed over the many years in my life that people who accept responsibility are the people who are making the most of their lives.

> **Discovering your freedom of choosing your own attitudes towards life's challenges will affect your rate of success and happiness in life enormously.**

Accepting responsibility is accepting challenge, and accepting challenges throws open the doors and windows through which glorious opportunities and achievements enter our lives. Many people are afraid to accept responsibility, which is akin to not taking risks because of fear of failure. However, to have tried and failed is no disgrace but not to have tried is disaster.

Let your children know that it is a rough road that leads to heights of greatness. You could be their role model and you will be surprised how much the children learn from you and who you are. They inspect you when you are not noticing it, they listen to you speak, and watch your every gesture and movement. They notice the minutest things about you, how you treat your employees, how you deal with business associates, how you behave in public and how you react in tough moments. You are, in fact, a walking, talking example to your children whether you are aware of it or not.

Exposing your children to the harsher realities of life (while protecting them from harm) is an excellent self-taught education that goes far beyond what can be learnt in school and college. One excellent way is to encourage your children to read good books, outside their syllabus. It is a pity that our children are so exposed to sleazy television programmes and mindless activities such as video games and computer that take up most of their free time.

Accepting responsibility is accepting challenge, and accepting challenges throws open the doors and windows through which glorious opportunities and achievements enter our lives.

As a responsible parent, and with the help of your spouse, discipline your children so that they learn to eliminate mindless activities. It is no wonder that so many children, especially those from rich families, are so unhappy and 'so bored' all the time. As they grow older, they begin to find everything 'meaningless'. This is because there is a serious lack of goals and they have had no training in tapping their own potential. The growing years are the most creative years and these children are not using their minds and inherent potentials at all. Encourage them to develop latent talent, whether in music, art, sport, language skills, or acting — whatever it may be. You are not at this stage preparing them for their future careers so much as moulding them to be better and more balanced human beings.

In school, they may be taught to memorise huge amounts of facts. At home, they play endless games or watch inane television programmes. While they are still young, expose your children to the wide and wonderful world of books, music, art and good theatre. After all, man does not live by bread alone. By exposing your children to a little bit of all the good things that the world has to offer in its varied forms, you are showing them the road map to find endless treasures later in life. You are truly then, teaching them how to fish. Just as the ocean has millions of varieties of marine life, the world has millions of mysteries waiting to be solved and thousands of wonderful things to see and learn about.

The pond and the ocean

As your children grow up, seeing and learning, reading and observing, their universe too grows. When you teach your children 'to fish' you are not simply teaching them the means and techniques of survival, you are introducing them to life. In your grandfather's time, the world was a smaller place because lives revolved around simpler routines and very few people had the opportunity to travel or communicate with the larger, outside world. Imagination played a very big role in life those days and even in our days. Fostering imagination in children today has become a tough job because so much 'wonder' is ready-made and available at the push of a button. None of this wonder though comes from the child's capacity to imagine, so after a while, the ability to imagine things dies. This is the single greatest tragedy of our times, because imagination is the *only* foundation of future wonder and progress.

Your children's world has shrunk already, given the fantastic developments in information technology. But the IT world is a 'virtual' or 'make-believe' world, not the real flesh and blood world we live in. It has its own uses and big advantages, but it still does not and should not represent the real world. The children see the world and real time news on television from everywhere in the world. Remember on September 11, 2001, when the twin towers came crashing down in New York city, every child saw it happening, again and again. That is how small the world has become today.

Ironically, the same child who is closely familiar with US sports and film stars' personal lives may know very little about his own father or grandparents' lives. They may know the nicknames of French or American fashion models but have no clue about the next door neighbour's name. This is not a healthy trend. Responsible parents should step in and correct whatever is unhealthy or unbalanced in their children's lives.

There is something you can do to correct the balance. Tell your children stories about how you grew up, anecdotes about your childhood, about your parents and brothers and sisters. Let them become familiar with the pond and let them also know about the ocean just beyond the horizon. Let the children understand their own culture and traditions, beginning within the family, and then moving out to embrace the social group and the nation and then humanity itself. This will give them a stronger sense of identity, an understanding of where they belong and who they are. It will teach them to respect others, both within and outside their own family, social group, nationality and finally the world. It will help them in adjusting their perspectives and to become more stable and sensible human beings. While you are encouraging them to learn more, you will end up learning a great deal yourself.

The crucial years

Raising your children is one of the most important and difficult jobs that you will ever have. It is a job that you have to accept once the children are born, whether you like it or not, with very little experience and no formal training. As a successful businessman, you may have wealth, power and freedom, far more than at least 90 per cent of the population in this country.

Growing up is a difficult time for all children, more so for children who will be inheriting material success, especially if they are not prepared to accept the responsibilities that go with it.

How do you teach your grown-up children and then your grandchildren responsibility, both financial and personal? No matter how one defines 'rich', which is really a relative term, the fact is that as children of a successful businessperson, they have some privileges and resources that most children don't. You are, after all, raising rich and privileged children. But the wealth is not a windfall, you didn't win a national lottery, you earned every rupee of it and your children must be taught to view it as such and learn how to manage it responsibly. And your responsibility is to prepare them to shoulder theirs.

One successful method that some enlightened American business families have followed and that at least two business families I know in India have adapted to suit them is actually very simple.

When your child is between 12–15 years, you may open a bank account for him. A simple savings account that issues cheques, preferably with the child's name printed on them? Watch your child's look of awe and excitement when he receives the first cheque-book. Now, your spouse and you, with the active participation of the child, have to decide how much money goes into the account and what it will pay for. The best thing is to include some of the necessities and little extras such as clothes, shoes, music cassettes, movies, eating out with friends, games and so on. With each family and individual child, these items will differ and some degree of flexibility is needed that can be democratically worked out. What you then do is to put in the fixed amount

> **Growing up is a difficult time for all children, more so for children who will be inheriting material success, especially if they are not prepared to accept the responsibilities that go with it.**

into your child's account every month and he becomes responsible for paying the bills and keeping an account of what all is being spent.

Now watch what happens. It will be a whole new learning experience for the child when he is 'spending his own money' to actually pay for things that he had taken for granted before. He will make a few mistakes at first (and must bear the consequences — you absolutely MUST NOT compromise and rush to help him out), over-spending, buying things at a higher cost, forgetting to pay a bill and so on. But soon he will start to become wise. He will learn to economise in areas he can manage to do without, he will find out where he can get 'cheaper deals', he will understand the value of quality, of economy and frugality all at the same time. No textbook can prepare him for these lessons, he would have had to learn the hard way later in life. Over and above what he learns in managing money, he will learn to respect its value. As he grows older, he will appreciate things like not economising on quality for long lasting items because it works out more expensive in the end, and he will learn how to balance his accounts as an adult.

Of course there's much more to raising children than teaching them financial responsibility, although it is a very important aspect that should not be ignored. What you are doing is to prepare your children for a way of life. And this preparation should begin in the crucial, formative years.

Discipline does not mean being strict

I am always surprised when successful people equate

discipline with being strict or harsh. The basic lesson of discipline is the knowledge that certain things that have to be done, cannot be postponed, that right is right and wrong is wrong and that there is no substitute for integrity. We have to set standards, by our own behaviour and actions that the children can see and relate to unconsciously. If you and your spouse do not follow certain basic disciplines, you cannot expect your children to learn them.

Of course, the chances are that your life is fairly disciplined, otherwise you would not be a successful businessperson. You cannot afford to stay in bed late or make and then miss appointments, you cannot take a break from work just because you 'don't feel up to it today', and so on. You probably get up early or at least at the same time every morning, leave for work on schedule and work until late and you most probably go to work even when you don't feel very well.

In their growing years, the children have certain built-in routines that can become excellent lessons in discipline. Like you, they too have a job, that of students. This is where you can start your lessons. Schoolwork and all the extra-curricular activities that the child is engaged in should be followed in a disciplined manner. From the time the child wakes up, until he goes to bed, certain strict routines should be followed about how he spends his time. After school hours, it is important to create a fixed time for study, for games, for watching television (including monitoring the programmes he is permitted to watch), dinner, chit-chat on the phone with friends and so on. Homework should be finished every day and the responsibility should gradually become the child's alone. If he goofs up, let him endure the punishment his teacher metes out.

Discipline will then move on to his social activities. How he behaves with domestic help, how he treats elders, how he shares his belongings with his siblings and friends. He may pick up abusive language from all sorts of places and must be taught to curb his tongue. He will learn all about bullies and bullying and must be taught never to pick fights with those who are smaller than him. All children get into playground scuffles and must be taught to deal with these things on their own. It is absolutely *wrong* for parents to enter into the fray and use their power to intimidate other children because their own children got involved in a fight and came home crying. If you give them the impression that you will be there to bail them out, they will carry this into their adult years and expect you to bail them out of their serious problems later on. This happens all the time. Children must learn very early that if they get into a fight, they will get hurt and will hurt others.

Too many kids from rich homes are over-protected and under-disciplined. All that happens in the end is that they grow into wayward adults, with huge egos and no sense of social responsibility. They believe they can get away with anything because their rich father or mother will 'take care' of things. So many tragedies have taken place because of this belief and also because the children never learnt the value of discipline.

Another area where many parents give in to their childrens' whims and fancies is in their food habits. In most well-to-do homes, children are extremely fussy about their food. They will not eat this or that, or are fed on the most unhealthy food because "at least something is going into their stomachs." I know of one mother who gives her two-year-old child several glasses of Coca-Cola everyday and solid food comprises chips, Maggi noodles and chocolates. When I mentioned the unhealthy quality of food the child was getting, the mother, an educated woman, said, "What to do, my child won't eat anything else!" Imagine! As if the two-year-old would know about chips and Coke if the mother had not got her into this ridiculous habit in the first place.

Giving in to children at all times is the worst thing you can do to them. Children must learn, early in life, that they can't get everything they want at all times. They must learn to cope with boredom, frustrations and the grim sides of life. Otherwise, they simply collapse as adults or turn to crime to get what they want or to drugs to forget their frustrations.

Respect and love

Along with a sense of responsibility and discipline, you need to teach your children the basis of love, which is respect. Love cannot exist without respect and usually, respect is accompanied by love although not always. When I use the term love I am referring to that wonderfully liberating feeling we all feel towards whom we value most. Romantic love is another thing altogether. The love that we can teach our children is that universal love that goes with respect. It can be towards the family, towards family values, towards knowledge and learning, towards nature's free gifts, and most importantly towards one's self. To love yourself is to respect your essential being. If you do not learn to love yourself, you become incapable of loving anyone or anything else. This is a simple and universal truth.

Love begets love and respect attracts respect and vice versa. If you respect your child as a special, unique human being that you are privileged to have with you to love and teach and care for, your child will not need to be 'taught' how to love and respect. She will be imbibing it on a daily basis. If you are disrespectful to elders in the family, you can bet your children will pick it up automatically. If you are rude to your spouse in front of your children don't expect them to respect either of you. They may not openly express their disrespect but in their hearts, they will feel it, especially if you make a habit of it. It's true that everyone quarrels once in a while, but parents should keep their quarrels within the privacy of their bedrooms and not allow children to be party to it.

Love cannot exist without respect and usually, respect is accompanied by love although not always.

In a home where parents show a distinct love and respect towards each other, children feel secure and the occasional loss of temper or even an open fight can be accepted by them as a part of relationship that is essentially sound and good.

How you treat others will rub off on your children. It is very distressing to see a nine-year-old kid abusing the driver or the cook or the chowkidar in language that would make a soldier blush. He is simply imitating his dad without, in most cases even knowing the meaning of what he says, but it is a terrible lesson he picks up in social interaction.

We cannot become teachers overnight nor will our children learn everything overnight. These processes are lifelong pursuits. By starting early and concentrating on the right lessons, we create the foundation to build the future, both our own and our children's. With mutual love and respect, a sense of discipline and responsibility, happy mealtimes and sharing both jokes and serious issues openly, we create strong family bonds and a natural desire to do the best for each other. Given this bond and a commitment to the children that their welfare comes first, the chances are that your children will grow up to become good human beings and possibly worthy heirs to your business.

> **How you treat others will rub off on your children. It is very distressing to see a nine-year-old kid abusing the driver or the cook or the chowkidar in language that would make a soldier blush.**

When outsiders become insiders

You have brought up your children well but the time will come for them to marry and bring in spouses who will become new family members. Beyond making a thorough background check of the bride or groom, there is no way to predict the dynamics that will develop in the new relationships that a marriage brings about. A new entrant to the family would automatically create some major shifts within the family. He or she will bring in values, attitudes and perspectives along with his/her physical presence into the new home. It is bound to cause some ripples after the honeymoon is over.

Just as with your own children, it is important that the new daughters/sons-in-law quickly learn about your family values and traditions so that they can adjust themselves and learn to fit in. If they are not too rigid and are open to small adjustments, they will soon learn, both about your business and the family and the relationship between the two.

In India, some business families arrange the marriages of their daughters in a manner that will promote the business. So often the son-in-law enters the family and becomes a director in the family business. It is a kind of trade-off instead of a dowry in some cases and may even include a few compromises.

In one Agarwal family I know, the son-in-law came from a decent, well-to-do family, but was a secret alcoholic (not so uncommon as we would wish). The parents of the bride had chosen the family but failed to find out about this habit of the son until it was too late. By the time they realised the truth, after about four months, the son-in-law was already made a director of the company and was not in the least interested about things like responsibilities and respect and so on. Worst of all, the daughter of the family had conceived but was already showing the strain of being married to a man who preferred his bottle and his buddies to his new bride.

The family was in a major fix but the father was no fool either. He knew that he had two choices. One, he could arrange for a divorce and an abortion (since the pregnancy was still within safe limits) and call it quits. God knows he had sufficient grounds for this decision. Two, he could take on the responsibility (and burden) of reforming his son-in-law. Mr. Agarwal chose the second option. Using respect, love and a bit of emotional blackmail (he was justified in using whatever method he did, because his daughter's future depended on it), he actually succeeded. Today, Rahul Gupta, the son-in-law, is a responsible father, a decent husband and a serious business partner.

In the case of a daughter-in-law, it is the mother-in-law who plays a stronger role. Relationships are a two-way thing. A good daughter-in-law makes for a good mother-in-law and vice-versa.

In a business family, however, the daughter-in-law is more than your son's wife, she will be the mother of the heirs to the business. It is so easy to make an enemy instead of an ally of a new entrant to the family without even trying too hard. By treating your daughter-in-law with respect, kindness, love and trust, you will gain reciprocal feeling from her. If you are cold towards her or constantly find fault with her, she will grow distant and after a while begin to hate you. When the children are born, she will unconsciously or purposefully pass on the same sentiments to them. In the end you will be the loser because no matter how loyal your son is, he will start to feel uneasy and helpless in a situation of divided loyalties and will finally settle the matter in favour of his wife and children. So, treat your daughter-in-law like "Lakshmi" and she will bring in peace and happiness and wealth and joy. Your son-in-law cannot take the place of your sons but deserves the same respect and affection. Eventually, he will become part of your extended family and will be directly responsible in building the dynasty.

Change is inevitable and if your business is to survive you and provide for your children and their children, adaptive growth is essential.

Success is a Journey, Not a Destination | 6

Preparing a blueprint for daily success

When you started out in your venture you were in business for yourself but now, with success, you have earned a certain security, a status in society. You have made it to your 'dream goal'. Have you then reached your final destination?

After years of denying yourself, cutting corners and making sacrifices, you may suddenly discover that you have all the wealth that you require, and now you can *relax.* Almost everything you want, can be yours, your children can have the best and so can your spouse. Usually, self-indulgence would not come immediately, because you have got into the habit of saving and cutting corners for too long, but it will come, as it does to so many others in the same situation.

Entering a new world

As the fruits of success begin to show, the family begins to move into different relationships, a better house, club memberships, bigger cars, and so on. The children too acquire expensive tastes.

At this stage, you need to assess where you are placed in your business? Is it a success, making money on its own momentum set up by you earlier. What are your choices? You are now probably in your 50s, and having worked very hard through your life, you are tired and need rest. Most businesspeople at this stage become secretive again and fearful about projecting their wealth and look around for security to guard their wealth from rivals, suppliers, likely competitors, and from their relatives. And not so surprisingly, most businesspeople choose at this stage to call it a day. There is too much hard work involved. Except for those areas that manage on their own, just as they are, the owner resists growth because growth involves accepting change. After all, the world keeps changing. The whole business of computers, of the flourishing new language of hi-tech terminology may be foreign. You may believe that you are too old to learn and don't have to really. The office has all the new gadgets, but others operate them and you still stick to old techniques, whether in accounting or dictating letters.

This is a perfectly understandable situation, but there is a dangerous delusion behind it. The founder businessperson imagines that because he doesn't want to change (it is too tiring), change won't happen. Actually *a profound change is taking place* in you if you feel this way.

Building a successful business is a major accomplishment that you undertook in your youth and made a huge success of over the years. You worked against all odds, fought and won battles on a daily basis, adapted to the changing marketplace and made many shifts in your own life and practices. Not wanting to change is a change in itself from your earlier dynamic self.

Change, however, is inevitable and if your business

is to survive you and provide for your children and their children, adaptive growth is essential. Once again, you may have two choices. You may stop altogether at this successful stage when money is coming in on its own, or accept change.

Planning for change

If you have kept the family and employees abreast of what has been happening during the growing years in the business, you are already well set. But, *close to 90 per cent of business people* do not simply have the time or the inclination to do this. The children have grown up and may be apart, the employees simply do their 'jobs' and do not have the foggiest idea about the working of the business. Not even your accountant knows how much is spent or earned, because you have at least two accounts, the real one and the one for public knowledge. This is common practice.

Unfortunately, at this stage of your life, when your energy levels are down, you find yourself isolated and terribly lonely.

It is impossible to alter your energy level in the prime of your life to keep up with the demands at the workplace. Instead, what you can do is to learn to change from being a *doer* to being a *teacher.* But this is not easy, particularly for a businessperson, because, in your own mind, you may think, there's nobody else who can do things as well as you can, where business is concerned.

But the time has come to learn to look for people (they do exist you know), who can indeed do things well and perhaps better than you, and not to be so fearful of the future. It is time to learn to accept a little bit of 'dust', and this reminds me of a story.

In my time, I grew up in a household where the women were proficient in household chores. As a student, I had my own desk and my mother dusted and cleaned my desk and chair and tidied up my books and instruments everyday (because I was too lazy to do it myself). I always had a neat, tidy, dust-free desk.

Then, I grew up, started to work and got married. I had my own desk in my new home and papers began to collect. At first, my wife had a lot of time and everything continued as before. After a few years, the children came along one by one and she had hundred new jobs to do. I had never got into the habit of keeping my own desk neat at home, and was initially too busy to notice the occasional dust that would collect in corners. One day when I did notice, I was shocked! This was not how my mother did things. I brought up the subject with my wife, who by now was busy bringing up our three children with all the attending responsibilities. Homework, school programmes, health care, supervising the domestic help, cooking, cleaning and all the thousand things that make a household run efficiently. She took care of everything, while I was busy with my work outside the house. But that corner of dust on my desk was getting on my nerves so I drew a heart on it with my wife's name inside.

She, being a very intelligent lady, simply left that circle of dust and its message there, staring at me. It took me almost one month but I began to think of the message it sent me. I eventually realised that no house can be entirely dust-free. Things can always be improved, but at some point happiness needs some mutually acceptable level of dust. No one and nothing is perfect.

So, sooner or later someone will have to do the job you have been doing all your life. Usually, what stops you from delegating responsibilities to others, relaxing and finally retiring with peace of mind, is your inability *to accept some dust.* You can either make sure that your heirs and successors profit from your experience and knowledge or you can make sure they don't. It's entirely up to you. Because how they actually do the job, assuming they get the chance, is really up to them.

Timely action helps avoid dangers

A successful and growing business has management needs that are continuously changing. Survival requires change and change demands constant and competitive management. You may believe that things would become better tomorrow and these problems would go away if you only wait a few years (while your son grows up, or you find the perfect manager). Unfortunately, time simply passes and time has this quality of making simple problems grow complex with its passage.

You can either make sure that your heirs and successors profit from your experience and knowledge or you can make sure they don't. It's entirely up to you.

You have already reached a stage of 'perfection' in your mind, with your business making pots of money on its own while you relax. You now look forward to this as a 'permanent' reward for all your years of hard work. But this is a false dream. It is not workable because you are not the kind of person to simply stop work and drink cocktails in clubs half the day. You succeeded because of your need to build and achieve something. This internal drive doesn't simply disappear because you have become successful or grown older.

On the other hand, even if you accept inactivity and aimlessness to a large extent, and can continue to milk your already successful business — there is a limit to how much it will give and for how long. Even the most productive cow will need to take a rest after a while and its level of production will go down and eventually dry up.

A successful family-owned business is a better investment in these days of fluctuating markets than gold, diamonds, stocks and shares, bonds and debentures and even, as recent events have proved, real estate. It represents *earning* power, but that earning power will continue only if time, effort, dedication and commitment are invested in the *continuity* of the business and therefore, in the people who will make the business work when the founder is no more.

One thing you have to agree upon is that your future and the future of your business lies with your heirs and successors, whether they are from your own family or not. This means that you have some confidence in the future and are willing to take a risk on your chosen successors in whom you have faith.

A calculated risk

What better risk is there than taking on something we understand and are familiar with? What better risk can there be than one that we can influence, both through our direct efforts and through our ability to transfer our knowledge and experience to others who also understand? This kind of risk is called an educated or calculated risk. And it is this kind of risk that the survival of a successful business demands. If such risks are not taken, the business will surely die. It would either fail, be liquidated or get sold. And along with it, will disappear the earning power, the freedom and the opportunity that took us, business founders, so much hard work to build.

You may have earned the right to stop *doing* after a point of time but you have also earned the responsibility to *teach* others so that your business can continue to grow.

> **You may have earned the right to stop *doing* after a point of time but you have also earned the responsibility to *teach* others so that your business can continue to grow.**

This is what I mean by preparing a blueprint for success, creating a map that defines the future and working on success as a daily achievement rather than a destination that you reach at the end of a journey.

If you aim for
the stars, you land
on the moon, you
get somewhere!
If you stand on the ground,
with the crowds all around,
you get nowhere!

7 Persevere with Passion

Lage raho, lage raho, lagan se

Make your successors *a part of the solution*

You have known all along but by now understand the *urgency* and *extreme importance* of being prepared for the future. You have to prepare your successors to take over smoothly at a later date, in a manner that is best for the business.

You will need to teach your children or whoever your successors are going to be (a bright nephew, a younger brother, or an adopted heir, for example) some crucial things. This is to make them a part of the future and a part of the solution that you seek.

To begin with, we will divide the lessons into six easy parts and then continue onwards.

Lesson # 1

The rich don't work for money

Money is a form of power. But what is more powerful than money is financial education. Money is just another commodity, it comes and goes, but if we have the knowledge about how money works, *we gain power over money* and can build wealth. Positive thinking is a wonderful attitude, but positive thinking alone does not work. Not everyone who goes to school and does brilliantly in academics learns how to make money work, because this is not taught as a subject. So people spend their entire life working for money *and not in making money work for them.* This is a common truth we rarely sit and think about.

After the industrial revolution, most world economies changed. Machines made work easier, production faster and factories employed people in large numbers. Today, there are thousands of jobs available. This system makes our consumer-oriented society work. People wake up in the morning, go to work, and return home in the evening, day in and day out. At the end of the month, they get their pay-cheque and are happy. Money plays such an important role in our lives, that we live in terror of not having any. This works very well for employers because they know they will always have people to work for them for money.

As people begin to earn money, they also want more. Two emotions guide them. Fear and greed: fear comes from wanting security and greed comes from simply wanting more. Now, the fear of being without money motivates people to work harder and harder and then as the rewards start increasing, greed or desire sets in and people start thinking and dreaming about all the wonderful things that money can buy. And then, a pattern is set. The pattern of getting up, going to work, paying the bills, going to work, paying the bills... so that their lives are run forever by these two emotions, fear and greed. Offered more money, the cycle continues as spending increases (a better car, more expensive dining, designer label clothes and so on). This is the rat race.

Is there another way to look at earning money? After

all, whether a salaried worker or a businessman, poor or rich, we are all concerned with earning money. In fact, the very same emotions, greed and fear drive the rich as well. The richer you become, the more fearful and greedy you become. There are plenty of businesspeople who keep working even after they have plenty. They think that more money will eliminate their fear of not having enough, but in fact the fear simply gets worse. Many rich people become neurotic with their worries about securing their hard-won wealth and can't sleep at night.

What you have to teach yourself and your children is how to avoid falling into this trap.

Make your emotions work for you

Instead of allowing our emotions to rule us, we must learn to make our emotions work for us. It is ignorance about money that causes fear and greed. We have to confront our fear and greed by using our conscious minds to think about them and to find out what makes them drive our lives. Choosing what we think is right rather than giving into emotions blindly is one way out of this trap. Not being blinded by emotions, your mind then opens up and can spot opportunities that are otherwise lost to you.

> **Money does not solve problems. It can create problems. Intelligence solves problems.**

By learning to use their heads and their imagination, your children will identify opportunities to make money. This will in turn help them find more business opportunities so that very soon, the business will generate more money that will work for them, even when they are physically not present. Instead of working for money, money will be working for them.

Lesson # 2

Rich people acquire assets

Just as everyone needs to be computer literate, every businessperson needs to be financially literate.

It is unfortunate that people are focused too much on money and not on their greatest wealth, which is education alone. By education I do not mean formal education. If people are prepared to be flexible, keep an open mind and learn through experience, they will grow richer. Money does not solve problems. *Intelligence solves problems and produces money.* Money without financial intelligence is money soon gone.

Most people fail to realise that it's not how much money you make, it's how much money you keep that creates wealth. We have all heard of lottery winners who were poor, became rich and then poor again. We have also read about famous film stars and sons of rajas and noblemen who made or inherited millions and then died destitute.

A lot of youngsters aspire to be 'rich'. They are also impatient and want to get rich quickly. It is important, however, to be financially literate.

> **If you want to build the Empire State building you will first have to dig a very deep hole and make a strong foundation.**

If you want to build the

Empire State building you will first have to dig a very deep hole and make a strong foundation. If you are building a single-storey bungalow, you may have a 12-inch foundation. But most people dig a 12-inch foundation and build an Empire State building which quickly falls like a pack of cards, tumbling down with the first storm.

A deep and strong financial foundation is the first thing you need to give your children. Accounting is possibly the most boring subject on earth. It could also be the most confusing. But for those who want to be rich and remain rich, it is the most important subject they need to learn.

The potential business heir must know and understand the difference between an asset and a liability. Now you may think that this is too simple and that everyone understands this. You will be surprised to know that this is not at all true. *Rich people acquire assets. Others acquire liabilities* although they think they are assets. This idea is so simple that most people miss the point. The following statements are mantras for success. Have them printed in bold letters and stick them on a wall in front of you.

An asset is something that puts money in my pocket.

A liability is something that takes money out of my pocket.

Illiteracy, both in words and numbers, is the foundation of financial struggle. If people are having difficulties financially, there is something that they cannot read, either in numbers or words. Something is misunderstood. The rich are rich because they are more literate in different areas than people who struggle financially.

Today, there are many avenues open to become rich. In sports, television (acting, commercials, production, and so on) and even in careers like modelling, young people can make a great deal of money, very fast. But making a lot of money does not solve problems. It is *the mentality of the rich* that solves financial problems. When a young person without financial knowledge makes a lot of money, he quickly changes his lifestyle to 'show off' his wealth. Flashy cars, first class air travel, foreign vacations — all these frills — become top priorities. After a while, when the money stops coming in a huge gush, these people, having accumulated huge liabilities, find it hard to keep up and get into debt, spending, 'until the next cheque comes in'. And after some more time, well before they are in their prime, the money simply stops, and so do they, as if frozen in time! Money only accentuates the cash-flow pattern in a person's mind. Cash in, cash out is how 80 per cent of the people think. The more the income, the greater the expenditure.

Financial literacy or financial education is basically learning how to spend money — or, what to do after you make it. It means learning how to keep it longer and how to make it work for you. A person can be highly educated, professionally successful but financially stupid or illiterate. Such a person often works harder than he needs to because he has learned how to work hard but does not know how to make his hard-earned money work for him. So if you want to be rich and maintain your wealth, it's important to be financially literate.

Henry Ford I was neither very educated nor truly literate. He simply had a brilliant mind and was a financial genius. Remember that although education is an extremely important facet of a child's all-round development, education varies with different professions. A farmer, for example, must learn more about agriculture, climate, weather patterns, fertilisers, seeds and market trends than about grammar, syntax or public speaking. Appropriate education should be our goal. Teach your children simple things. Teach them about the meaning of assets and liabilities, about how to make money work for them to create wealth and above all teach them *how to mind their own business.*

Lesson # 3

Mind your own business

To become financially secure, a person must mind his own business, not someone else's. Everybody is familiar with McDonald's (the hamburger outlet in every city, in all the best shopping centres round the world). Here is a story.

Ray Kroc, the founder of McDonald's, was speaking to the MBA students at the University of Texas in 1974. He made a powerful presentation, giving an inspiring talk and at the end of it, students requested him to join them at their favourite bar for a glass of beer. Kroc graciously accepted. When they all settled down, he asked them, "What business

> **Remember, that although education is an extremely important facet of a child's all-round development, education varies with different professions.**

am I in?" Everyone laughed because they thought he was just joking. No one answered, so he asked, quite seriously, once again, "What business am I in?" The students laughed again, but one of them bravely answered, "Who in the whole world doesn't know that you are in the hamburger business Kroc."

Kroc chuckled and replied, "That is what I thought you would say. Ladies and gentlemen, I'm not in the hamburger business. My real business is real estate." He then explained to the spellbound group that although his primary business focus was to sell hamburger franchises, what he never lost sight of was the location of each franchise. He knew that the real estate and its location was the most significant factor in the success of each franchise. Basically, the person that bought the franchise was also paying for, or buying the land under the franchise for Kroc's organisation.

McDonald's today is the largest single owner of real estate in the world, owning more than the Catholic Church (headquartered in Vatican City, Rome, with properties in every part of the world).

The message here is: *mind your own business.* Financial unhappiness is often the result of people working all their lives for someone else. College education teaches students necessary skills to pursue the profession of their choice. But these skills are good only for people to go out and get a job. Even when doctors or architects go into private practice, they face serious financial challenges, no matter how much money they make. There is a big difference between a profession and a business but many people confuse the two.

Kroc was very clear on the difference between his profession and his business. His profession was 'selling'. But his business was the accumulation of *income-producing real estate.*

The main reason why the middle and upper-middle class are financially conservative, which means they cannot afford to take risks, is that they have no financial foundation. They have to play it safe. In a time of financial crisis, if they lose their jobs, many of them find that even their greatest asset, a house or a flat, costs more than they can afford. After all, property taxes have to be paid! And the property, if it is self-used, does not bring in any income. Then their car depreciates in value every year and needs more and more in maintenance costs. Without job security, they have nothing to really fall back upon. A single major illness can wipe them out completely. And if they had to take a loan to buy their house and their car, and then lost their job, their problems just magnify.

Mind your own business. Financial struggle is often the result of people working all their lives for someone else

So what are real assets? Real assets fall into several different categories but all of them should generate an income.

1. *A business that does not require one's presence. One owns it but it is managed or run by other people. If one has to work there, it's not a business, it's a job.*
2. *Stocks and shares.*
3. *Mutual funds.*
4. *Income-generating real estate.*

5. *Royalties from intellectual properties such as music, books, patents and so on.*
6. *Anything that has value, produces an income and has a ready market (e.g. gold, diamonds, works of art, a fleet of cars or trucks).*

The best thing about money is that it works 24 hours a day and can work for many generations. As your cash flow increases, you can buy luxuries. An important difference between the successful and the average person is that the successful person buys his luxuries last while others buy them first. These days, when salaries have escalated and top-level managers make a huge packet of money, you see them imitating the rich and even behaving like them. The women shop only for designer labels and French perfumes and the men let the Scotch, champagne and caviar flow freely at very stylish parties hosted on their terraced homes (rented by the company at huge costs). In areas of business, such as advertising and the many dotcom companies that sprang up and hired very smart, young men and women — a single quarter of recession took away thousands of jobs! So many sand castles were built and destroyed within a year or two. What these people do is to buy luxuries from the money earned with their blood, sweat and tears. What the rich do is earn money with blood, sweat and tears and *then invest that money* and let it earn for itself, by itself. Then with the interest earned, they buy a luxury item as a reward for themselves. Nothing is lost this way, because the capital is still intact and still earning money. That is true luxury.

After you have taken the time to invest your money

and built your business, you are ready to add the magic touch — the biggest secret of the rich. It is the reward that you and your children will get at the end of the road after minding 'your own business'.

Lesson # 4

Taxes and corporate power

Have you heard the story of Robin Hood of Sherwood forest in England? Many of our Bollywood films have a Robin Hood theme where the hero robs the rich to give to the poor. How many times have we heard the sentiments that the rich should pay for this or that? Or that the rich should pay more in taxes and give to the poor?

This idea of Robin Hood has caused more harm and grief to the poor than any good. The reality is that it is the salaried classes, especially those in the higher income bracket, that pay most of the taxes that the government collects. This collected pool of money is meant to take care of the poor and to help build national infrastructures. In India, the government in its wisdom had also 'nationalised' many organisations and built some, so that employment could be created and given to a larger number of people. It meant that many jobs were simply 'created'. We all know how well this worked out. Public sector employees had less accountability but had total job security (they could not be sacked unless they committed a crime — not working was not considered a crime). Over a period of time, most of these PSUs became sick and now are being sold to the private sector.

The government is the single largest employer in the country. It is its job to spend allocated funds to hire more people. It also subsidises many items such as foodgrains, petrol, kerosene and LPG. Why is it done? The simple truth is that the government is run on committees and boards and endless meetings and almost no accountability. Take, for instance, India's foodgrain production. Forty-three per cent of our foodgrains are wasted (i.e. almost half of our produce) due to poor warehousing facilities. Either the rats eat them or rain and other natural conditions destroy them. We are one of the most wasteful nations in the world and one of the poorest. This is because money management has never been our strong point. Yet, it is money that makes everything possible and everyone desires money. The rich are envied because they have it. The poor are pitied because they don't.

To be a great manager in any venture, education of tax laws is important.

Some of India's largest industrial houses pay so little tax that you would think they were bankrupt. Actually what these rich corporates do, is to hire the smartest legal brains educated in taxation law to find ways to save taxes. The money saved is often distributed to shareholders and to employees by way of bonuses and perks. Rather than pay the government that will either waste or mismanage the money, the rich build their own schools and hospitals and often their own townships.

The rich have the money power to save money that the salaried classes don't. Although the same information is available to everyone, very few actually find the time or the interest to use it. A businessperson will think ten times before parting with ten rupees for a kilo of potatoes because he thinks it's too much and can get it cheaper elsewhere while a salaried man would be too embarrassed to bargain.

Ours is a free and democratic country that has laws to protect each citizen equally. The rich make full use of this, while most salaried people are foggy about these laws (I'm talking of tax laws) and don't find out enough about the deductions they are legally entitled to. Nor do they plan their spending according to the tax shelters available to them. It is expensive not to know the law because you end up paying when you don't have to.

Of course the corporate houses are able to pay much less in taxes because they are permitted to spend (on salaries, buying more assets, a variety of expenses etc.) before they are taxed while salaried people pay tax at source. But even here there are many, many ways and means of saving money.

> **The rich have the money power to save money that the salaried classes don't.**

Lesson # 5

The rich create money

While I was in the USA once, visiting my son Vijay and his family, I happened to watch a TV programme on the history of a young man named Alexander Graham Bell. The story began when Bell had just invented and patented his invention, the telephone. He was having some cash flow problems because the demand for his new invention was so strong. Needing a bigger company, he then went to the giant of his time, Western Union and asked if they would buy his patent and his tiny company. He wanted just $100,000 for the whole package. The president of Western Union laughed at his face and turned him down as a nut. The rest is history because a multi-billion dollar industry emerged and AT&T was born.

The same evening, I watched the news and a different kind of story. This was in the late 1980s and America was going through a recession. On the news was a story of one more local company that was downsizing and sacking its employees. The camera focussed on one such 'terminated' manager, about 45 years of age, with a wife and two kids who was begging the guards to let him talk to the owners of the company. He had just bought a house on loan and was afraid of losing it. The entire country must have been watching and feeling sorry for the man.

I began to think about it. Having been an employee myself, before I became a self-employed person after retirement, I am familiar with both the worlds. Inside each one of us is a brave, brilliant and daring character. On the other hand, we could also go down on our bended knees and beg if the situation came to that. I realised that it is excessive fear and self-doubt that makes us beg. Often in the real world, it is not the smart ones that get ahead but the bold.

In my personal experience, the business potential inside you requires both technical/practical knowledge as well as courage. If fear is too strong, the genius within you is silenced. Learn to be bold, to take risks, to let your genius convert fear into power and brilliance. I have come to realise that when it is a question of money, most people prefer to play safe. If someone asks me, "Why should I take risks or why should I bother developing my financial IQ when I can hire the best financial brains?" I tell them, "Just to have more options."

There are huge changes coming up. We can all see how fast things are moving these days. In the times to come, there will be hundreds of people like Aziz Premji and Bill Gates and hugely successful companies like Gates' Microsoft and Premji's Wipro will be created every year all over the world. It has already started happening and the pace will just keep increasing. And, there will also be bigger bankruptcies, layoffs and downsizing.

Tell your children how fortunate they are to be living in such an exciting time of turmoil and fantastic growth opportunities, in so many new directions. Before Independence, land was the precious commodity, after Independence, it was industry, today it is information. The person who has timely information today has the wealth. In fact, in more ways than one, information is wealth.

I find so many people struggling, holding on to old ideas, working harder and harder, wanting things to be the same way because they are afraid of change. In business, more than in anything else, old ideas are a liability. They are a liability because people fail to grasp that while that idea or way of doing something was an asset yesterday, *yesterday is gone.*

In my personal experience, the business potential inside you requires both technical/ practical knowledge as well as courage.

Limiting your options is the

same as hanging on to old ideas. And financial intelligence means simply having more options. If opportunities are not coming your way, what else can you do to improve your financial position? If an opportunity falls in your lap and you have no money and the banks turn you down, what else can you do to get the opportunity to work in your favour? Suppose you have invested on the intuition of making money and the idea fails, how do you turn a lemon into millions? That is financial intelligence. What exactly is the meaning of intelligence? Intelligence is wisdom + knowledge. Make another poster of this three-word equation and hang it on your wall so that you can see it every day.

Wisdom + Knowledge = Intelligence

It is not so much what happens but how many solutions you can think of to turn a lemon into a million. It is how creative you are in solving financial problems.

Most people know only one solution (because it has been drummed into our heads since kindergarten): work hard, save money and these days, borrow.

The reason why you must teach your children and yourself to learn to increase financial intelligence is because you want your children to be the kind of people who create their own luck. Teach them to take whatever happens and make it better. Few people understand that luck is created, just as money is. If you wait for the 'right' things to happen, then it's like waiting for all the traffic lights to turn green from Nizamuddin to Faridabad before you start your car.

The single most powerful asset we have is our mind.

If it is trained well, it can create wealth in what seems an instant. (Actually this is true. Really rich people earn in millions every hour of the day, everyday, including holidays). This is wealth beyond the dreams of kings and queens a few hundred years ago. Equally, an untrained mind also creates extreme poverty that lasts several generations by teaching it to their families.

In this Information Age, money is increasing geometrically. A few people are getting ridiculously rich from nothing, just by ideas and agreements. If you go to the stock exchange, you will see what I mean. A hand signal, a blip on a computer screen and millions of rupees are transacted — without a rupee being exchanged. People buy and sell without money, just on an agreement. Such is the age we live in and it will change even more rapidly. Plastic money is already taking the place of cash and 'virtual' money will soon take its place.

The point I am making here is that investments come and go, the markets go up or down, economies improve and crash. The world is always handing you opportunities of a lifetime, every day of your life. We fail to see them. But they are there. There is money floating in the air, literally. And the more the world changes, the more technologies change, the more opportunities will be available for you and your family to be secure for generations to come.

> **If you wait for the 'right' things to happen, then it's like waiting for all the traffic lights to turn green from Nizamuddin to Faridabad before you start your car.**

Following is a list of a few important lessons you must teach your children:

1. *Inspire them to learn more.*
2. *Let them know that it is easy to build if the foundation is strong.*
3. *Show them that anyone can achieve great wealth.*
4. *Show them that there are many, many ways to achieve their goals.*
5. *Show them that making money is not rocket science and they can do it.*
6. *Eventually it is all a game. Sometimes you win, sometimes you lose.*
7. *There is always a risk, so learn to manage risk instead of avoiding it.*

Lesson # 6

Work to learn, don't work for money

The world is full of smart, educated and talented people. India has so many such young people. We meet them every day, because they are all around us. The other day, my car was giving me trouble so my driver stopped at a mechanic's shop in Khan Market. The mechanic, a young man, put his ear to the bonnet of the car after starting the engine and immediately knew what was wrong. He fixed the problem in two minutes and charged just Rs. 50 for the job. So much talent yet totally wasted!

About a year ago, a very smart young lady came to

interview me at my office. I had read some of the articles she wrote for her newspaper. She was a very good journalist, a good writer. She came on time and the interview went well. I offered her a cup of coffee and started to chat with her. She looked at me and said with a sad smile, "Someday, I want to be a bestselling author like you." I was touched and felt good. Then I asked her, "What keeps you from achieving your dream? You are a very good writer and have a great style."

She told me that she had written two novels and they were appreciated but went nowhere. So she keeps her job to pay her bills. Then she asked me if I had any suggestions for her.

I told her to take a course in sales. She was shocked and offended. "I have an M.A. in English Literature," she said, really upset by now, "and you want me to take a course in sales? I hate all sales people, all they want is money."

One of my books was lying on the coffee table and the cover said in bold, gold letters: Bestselling author, Promod Batra. I pointed it to her and said: "Books always say bestselling author not best writing author. I am a terrible writer. You are a great writer. You have a Master's degree and I have an MBA with a specialisation in sales. Put them together and you get both a bestselling and a bestwriting author." But she was too angry by now. "I will never stoop so low as to learn how to sell. People like you have no business writing. I am a professionally trained writer and you are a salesman. It's just not fair!"

Anyway, I apologised for speaking out of turn and she left in a mighty huff. The next month, her magazine carried a very good interview of mine.

I am constantly shocked at how little really talented and skilled people earn. Writers, doctors, engineers and such people struggle financially all their lives. This is because they are just one skill away from great wealth. I have already mentioned earlier that financial intelligence is a synergy or combination of knowledge in accounting, investing, marketing and law. And a classic example of this would be that young lady journalist.

If she learned the skills of sales and marketing, her income would jump dramatically. Look at it this way, no matter how great an artist or writer one may be, if you cannot 'sell' your work, you will not be known. There are many such 'great' artists, who remain undiscovered because they don't have the skills to market themselves. And there are many not so great artists (and writers, inventors, products or people in any walk of life) who become rich and famous, simply because they are skilled at public relations, sales and marketing.

When American writer Robert T. Kiyosaki, wrote his first book, he titled it: *If You Want to be Rich and Happy, Don't Go to School?* His publisher suggested he should change it to *The Economics of Education.* Kiyosaki told the publisher that with a title like that he would sell just two books. One to his family and one to his best friend and both would expect it for free. Kiyosaki was not against education, in fact he fought for legislation for changes in the American education system to make it more up-to-date. What he was trying to do with his title, was to create a controversy and public interest. Anyway, the title remained and the book sold very well (making both the writer and the publisher richer).

The famous painter Vincent Van Gogh is probably the best example of a great artist and a lousy salesman. I know that a lot of people are going to get upset with me for saying this, but it is the truth nevertheless. Van Gogh's paintings are worth multi-million dollars today and those who love art revere him. Yet, he was so poor while he was alive that his younger brother had to send him money for his food and art material. *He did not sell a single painting while he lived and died destitute.* His brother, who survived him, became rich and in time his brother's family became really wealthy. Van Gogh was too poor to even marry!

It is unfortunate that in India we make a virtue of poverty — so now we have millions and millions of people who are virtuous but so poor that some die from lack of basic things like food, medicine and shelter. I don't know where this philosophy came from. After all we have a whole system called *Artha Shastra* that teaches us since ancient times how to make *artha* or money. Everyone worships goddess Lakshmi, the deity of wealth.

In India, another problem is that everyone expects the government to do something, to improve the economic situation. The government's job is to govern or administrate, not to create jobs or wealth! That is something only creative individuals, like you and I, can do. You must put this thought in your children's minds so that the next generation does not go around expecting someone else, least of all the government, to do what *they* should be doing. Communist countries made a brave attempt to correct a serious social wrong in their times and tried to institutionalize entrepreneurship. It worked well in some ways but the basic theory was faulty and was proved wrong and you can see what happened in China and the USSR. The Chinese are now outsmarting the capitalist countries in free enterprise — just look at how their products are taking over in every market round the world!

It is not enough to create or manufacture a great product, and it is not enough to have a talent or a special skill in something, you have to manage your product/talent and then market it.

The main management skills needed for success are:

1. *Management of cash flow.*
2. *Management of systems, including yourself and your family.*
3. *Management of people or public relations.*

The most important *specialised* skills are sales and marketing. The ability to sell is the same as the ability to communicate properly. Therefore, to communicate with the right people in the right way and at the right time — be it a customer, client, employee, boss, wife or child — is the foundation of personal success.

A lot of people are afraid of sales and marketing because it means a lot of public speaking. They are mainly afraid of being rejected or ridiculed. But instead Of avoiding this essential confrontation, we have to learn to handle the fear and improve our skills in communication, both written and spoken. We have to learn to be good students because learning doesn't stop when we finish school or college — it is a process that continues through life. The better we are at learning, the better our lives would become. In addition to being good learners, sellers and marketers, we have to also learn how to teach our acquired wisdom so that we keep passing it on to our children, their children and to anyone else around us who wants to learn. To be really rich, we have to learn to give as well as receive. The world's richest men are also some of the most generous. The more money you make, the more you can give away, and surprisingly, the more money you earn! It's like a cycle. You get, give and get more! Giving is actually the secret of receiving.

Your children, who will have to learn how to live in dignity with wealth have to also learn how to maintain and increase that wealth. As I said earlier and cannot emphasise enough, education is the foundation for progress, provided it is the right kind of education. Encourage your children to know a little about a lot so that they have a wide base. Encourage them to surround themselves with people who are smarter than themselves and to bring smart people together to make a team. You know what I mean: *Andho ke duniya me kana raja* or, the one-eyed man is the king in a nation of blind men.

To communicate with the right people in the right way and at the right time — be it a customer, client, employee, boss, wife or child — is the foundation of personal success.

Lives of
great men all
remind us,
we can make our
lives sublime.
And, departing leave behind us,
footprints on the sands of time.

Management Mahamantra: Think. Ask. Do.

8

How to sew buttons on an ice cream

This book is meant to show how a business family should manage its relationships so that both the business and the family prosper, become happy and then continue this trend for several generations down the line. What *you* should be doing is creating a family guideline, building a family culture that can be continued. It would be continued because it would be successful and members of the growing family would see the sense of continuing the culture that made them happy and prosperous. I have shared with you some stories, some personal experiences and a lot of things that I have learned from others' lives. Now it is up to you to bring it all together and make it a part of enriching your family and your business.

Very little of what is said in this book will be new to you. The knowledge is there inside you, perhaps unexplored, perhaps unspoken, but it is there. What I have attempted to do is put it together and I have given those unspoken, subconscious thoughts a form and a structure. That is the beauty of books. A single good book can change a person's life altogether. It is like lighting a lamp in a dark cave and seeing the treasure hidden at the back. The treasure was always there but it needed the help of a lamp to discover it. Now, one could choose to see and then forget. See and then ignore. See and then complain that there is no time to dig out the treasure and use it. So long as all the treasures (knowledge, skills, talent) remain unused, unpolished and unsold, it is nothing but a collection of bright, shiny objects with which civilizations have grown, prospered and died. As adults, we need to think, ask and then do and I will gradually explain why.

The human mind is our greatest single treasure. No one can take it away from us. Even if we were to become prisoners of war, our bodies may be imprisoned, but our minds remain free. It is the human capacity to think that has created the wonders of the world and its worst catastrophes as well.

Thinking can be productive or destructive. Positive thinking takes you places while negative thinking (or worrying) keeps you tied up in chains. Then there is that other thing — lack of thinking. Many of us say or do things without thinking. Later, we are, regretful.

Thought is a product of the mind and its raw materials are learning, experience and imagination. What we cannot imagine, what we have not experienced or what we have not learned, we cannot think about. If our learning, experience or imagination is flawed, our thoughts will also be flawed. A child brought up without love, exposed to abuses (his experiences) and taught wrong things will grow up imagining that this is how things are and should be. He or she will grow up to be cold, brutal and criminal. A child who is taught good behaviour, exposed to a variety of healthy information and knowledge, loved and encouraged, will grow into a balanced adult. Although

Thought is a product of the mind and its raw materials are learning, experience and imagination. What we cannot imagine, what we have not experienced or what we have not learned we cannot think about.

neither of these outcomes are hundred per cent guaranteed, it is the rule and as in everything else in life, there are exceptions.

Thinking, before saying or *doing,* gives us the time to respond to something logically, reasonably and in a balanced manner. Your response to anything, if it is thoughtful, would have greater chances of being successful, smart or progressive. But sometimes, even our best thought-out actions or plans go wrong. And this usually happens because we lacked something, some information or knowledge, without which the best-laid plans could go wrong. And this brings us to the second point of the Mahamantra.

ASK

Have you noticed how children are constantly asking questions? Why, how, when, what, and then why, why and why again. Children are dynamos of learning. They ask hundreds of questions because they have a basic need to learn. Only learning can satisfy their endless curiosity about this wonderful world they discover themselves in. They want to know everything. Why this happens, how that works, what is the meaning of this, that or the other? Adults get fed up with these incessant questions sometimes (because they are so busy with their own lives) and may tell them a little, explain things hurriedly, or tell them to be quiet and go out to play. But children also learn while they are playing (thank heavens!), and in fact, their every waking moment is a process in learning.

Asking is one of the simplest tools of learning. Asking can involve questioning others who know more, reading books, travelling and learning new things that way, and so many other things. Asking is not confined to only questions that you voice to those physically near you. Ask Einstein, for instance, about his theory of relativity and he will answer you — in printed form, through his books or even through books written by others about his work. Asking is seeking answers and you can seek answers from the whole universe. Today, we are so fortunate that information comes to us in whatever form that suits us. For instance, Amar Chitra Katha comics are illustrated and highly simplified versions of huge works of literature that were originally written in very difficult Sanskrit. Most children have read them and thus know at least the basic Ramayana, Mahabharata and Panchatantra stories. I think they are absolutely wonderful!

Practically everything known in the universe, from the beginning of time, is quite easily available to us, in some form or the other today. All we need to do is seek this knowledge, all we need to do is ask the right questions. No one on earth can know everything about everything there is to know. Yet, for everything we *need to know* or want to know, the answer exists close at hand.

This reminds me of a story from the Panchatantra. It is called *The Lapwings and the Ocean.* A lady lapwing plump with eggs *asked* her husband to find a safer place to nest because they lived on the shores of the great ocean.

> **Asking is one of the Simplest tools of learning. Asking can involve questioning others who know more, reading books, travelling and learning new things that way, and so many other things.**

The male was a confident fellow and *asked* her to lay her eggs right there. *Now,* greedy ocean that was always looking for things to eat from the shore heard their discussion and waited till the lady lapwing had laid her eggs. The next day when she flew away for a few moments to stretch her tired wings, the ocean quietly stole the eggs.

When she returned to her nest and saw that her eggs were gone, the lady lapwing began to howl and cry and blamed her husband for choosing such a bad place for their nest. But the lapwing husband was not exactly a fool and he knew that he desperately needed help from someone who could tackle the mighty ocean. So, he *asked* for help from the king of birds, Garuda. Now Garuda was Lord Vishnu's vehicle and had certain powers and privileges in heaven. Garuda thought about the problem for a few moments and decided that he must now *ask* Vishnu to help his subject, the lapwing who had *asked* for his help and who he could not let down. Vishnu, who is the Lord of the oceans, roared at the ocean and commanded him to return the stolen eggs. The ocean trembled at his Lord's anger and meekly returned the eggs to the mother.

What this story portrays is the power of *asking.* The lapwing, a tiny bird, dared to ask his king, who in turn dared to ask God Himself, both seeking help to achieve final victory.

Sadly, as we grow older, leave alone asking others to help us, we gradually start to first lose our curiosity because we begin to believe we know all. What's left to see and know? As a successful businessperson, you may think 'enough now!' and actually feel it's too tiring to learn more. Do you know something? When you 'tire' your muscles by exercising, them, they become more efficient and then physical activities are *less* tiring — like climbing up and down stairs for instance. But allow your muscles to relax over a period of time and they become useless after a while. It is the same with the human brain. The more active it is, the more tireless it becomes and the more *easily* it will pick up information and knowledge. Things left unused will rust or decay and we all know that. So simple really, except that as we grow up, we become 'sophisticated' and think in complex terms — when all the basic truths, of life are very simple.

> **Being ignorant is not a crime, but defending it and keeping it that way certainly is.**

Don't ever feel embarrassed to ask. We feel that we will look 'stupid' if we ask a question, thereby revealing our ignorance. Being ignorant is not a crime, but defending it and keeping it that way certainly is. We can learn so much from our children, for instance, but we rarely bother to make the effort. Our children are one generation *ahead* of us. Therefore, they know some things that we never learned because that knowledge or information was not available to us. And our grandchildren would be a few steps ahead of our children — which is how it should be! Every moment of every day, the information and knowledge base in the world is increasing. Opportunities are linked with knowledge and as I mentioned earlier, in this information age, the person who has the latest and best information, has the cutting edge.

So ask, ask and ask, without embarrassment, with a curious mind, with the intention to learn. A rich man may not give you a ten-rupee note but he will gladly part with knowledge worth millions. People love to talk about their success, people love to teach others how to improve or how to become better, so why not take advantage of this? After all, you can only gain and let the loser remain with his closed mind if that is what he chooses. However, learning is not an end in itself. Learning must translate into something otherwise it is not going to resolve your problems. You have to put the learning or the answers to your questions to practical use. Your learning, in other words, is an asset that should bring in wealth. This wealth could take the shape of better relationships, better health, more happiness or more money. For this, you have to get to the next step.

> **People love to talk about their success, people love to teach others how to improve or how to become better, so why not take advantage of this?**

DO

Throughout this book you have picked up many small ideas and lessons that I hope will help you to think and ask more questions to achieve your goals in life. Having reached this stage of preparedness, you have to now show some action, and do that right now.

What this means is that you have to put your knowledge to practical use, translating thought and information into action. And this is the hardest part but it is also a challenge. The funny thing is everyone seems to 'know' and even 'understand' the best recourse to many problems that affect us, as individuals, groups, nations and the world but it takes a very special kind of person to *do* things.

Can you imagine how the world would be transformed if each one actually did what they should do? Let's call it the 'Power of One'. I recently heard this term in an advertisement promoting environmental responsibility. It made a great deal of sense to me. At the end of the day, all movements for reform start with the individual. You and I have to take that first step. Others can show us how or tell us why, but the doing is a personal choice each one of us has to make.

Like Arjuna, each one of us has inner courage but lack the will, confused by the many pushes and pulls working inside our heads and around us. Our relationships, our traditions, our fears and fantasies confuse us and cloud our judgment when a decision is needed. Each one of us needs a Krishna, by way of a good friend, a good book or a consultant of some kind who would show us the way. But even here, Krishna could help, but he could not *do* what Arjuna alone had to *do*.

Let us then put things in a nutshell, point by point, so that it is like a checklist that you could refer to for success. The details have been discussed earlier in this book and you could go back to whichever one you need to refer to, from time to time.

CHECKLIST OF THINGS TO DO

1. **Set your goals**

   Without setting your goals, you will not know which direction to take and will get muddled and lost along the way. Happiness is the primary goal. To reach that final goal, you will need other short and long-term goals that you must choose. Health and wealth, good relationships within the family, the children's upbringing are some of the goals you will want to keep in front of you.

2. **Dare to dream**

   Use your natural ability to dream and visualise a future (see it clearly in your mind's eye) for the next three generations. This vision will tell you what you need to do. Then plan for the future and put it into action.

3. **The family is your first priority**

   Your first and most important partner is your spouse. Make your partner an active participant in your dream. Share your dream with your spouse and your children, their spouses and later their children.

4. **Have courage in your dreams**

   You have a dream and you already have courage, otherwise you will not venture into the risks that all businesses carry with them. But now you must have courage in your dreams and don't allow anyone to tell you otherwise.

5. Be prepared

Change is the only constant. Change comes, whether we like it, accept it or lump it. Being prepared for change is the mark of a true visionary. Being prepared saves you money, time and heartbreak in the future.

6. Give importance to learning

Life itself is the most elaborate book and the best teacher. Learning does not end with schooling. Being a good, lifelong student will keep your mind active and in working condition, showing you the way out of the many pitfalls that you will encounter as you go along.

7. Open your children's minds

Besides the education they receive in school, encourage your children to value good things. Art, music, theatre, science, people, cultures and whatever else they want to learn about should be thrown open to them. This way your children will become balanced adults with a variety of knowledge.

8. Learn to trust people

Self-made men tend to distrust others, including family members. It is their greatest flaw. By building trustworthy people and surrounding yourself with such individuals, you will create a safety net around you. Life does not come with any guarantees, so you should make sure your business survives you to serve your family's future no matter what happens to you.

9. Invest time in your successors

If we assume that your children will be your successors, spend time with them now. It would be too late if you leave this for later. Share your experiences and wisdom with your children, they would value this and learn from this much more than anything else. Time spent with your successors is the best investment you will make in your life.

10. Teach your children well

Not all of us are good or natural teachers. So make it a part of your 'learning' exercise because you are your child's best teacher and the most important role model. It is *best* to start teaching your children when they are young, but *any* time is a good time to start this vital activity.

11. Build a strong foundation

Success and its continuity lies with you and your family. You cannot build a strong building with faulty material and you cannot build a tall building with a weak foundation. These are the basic laws of physics and of life. Make your children strong, expose them to the harsh side of life, shelter them but don't spoil them. *Shared* happiness, laughter, respect and love are the secrets of a strong family foundation.

12. Respect women

Despite the fact that women make up half the world's population, there is too much disrespect for women. Both men and women perpetuate this. It is time to learn and understand that women play a very important role in the world, a role, that men cannot quite substitute. Today, with women contributing in the workplace as well, we must sincerely correct our attitudes towards them.

13. Be responsible and teach responsibility

Only responsible people can make good things happen. All of us have certain basic responsibilities, towards ourselves and towards others. The more responsible we become, the more successful we are. As we grow older, our responsibilities grow and with it, our achievements.

> **Your love towards your children should be their anchor when they need one and their wings when they need to fly.**

14. Discipline is the basis of civilised life

All of civilised life would collapse without discipline. What we do, when and how, determine how well our lives are lived. Discipline, if taught to children when they are young, is not easily forgotten. Discipline should mark both our personal behaviour and our work ethics. Lack of discipline works out to be very expensive in the long run.

15. The immeasurable value of love

Love is caring and sharing but more than that, it is respect, trust, patience and compassion. It is the most valuable human virtue and can transform a criminal into a saint. Love gives children the inner security they need to grow true and strong. Your love should cover your children like an umbrella but should include their husbands, wives and children as they come along, Your love should be their anchor when they need one and should be their wings when they need to fly.

16. Opportunities versus risks

Learn to spot and use opportunities when they come but remember that they come with risks attached. You cannot have one without the other. Taking risks mean having a foundation of 'education' to cover them. An educated risk is almost always worth taking. Teach your children the same thing.

17. The value of financial intelligence

You are in business to make money and to create wealth. If money is what you would eventually accumulate, you must make financial literacy a continuing learning process. Most people earn to spend. You have to learn to earn to make your money earn for itself. This is the most valuable education you and your children can get. Financial intelligence comes with understanding and learning how to make money work for you rather than you working for money.

18. Build assets, not liabilities

Understand the real meaning of assets and liabilities so that each time you spend a rupee, you know whether it is an investment or an expenditure. An asset is something you spend on something that makes money for you. A liability is something that takes money from your pocket and bums a hole in it.

19. The importance of studying tax laws

You can hire twenty tax lawyers and specialists for this, but still it is your money that is bleeding away in unnecessary tax payments. Pay your taxes but don't give away what you don't have to. The only way you can control this is by acquiring some knowledge about tax laws and then cross-checking with your specialists and lawyers.

20. Learn to create money out of nothing

Whatever your line of business, once you become successful, what you have is a great deal of wealth. This wealth is also your 'produce' and can become a further source or raw material for more wealth. How do you make money out of nothing? By using your financial intelligence, entering that world where fortunes are made without actually 'spending' money. To avoid losing money, you need to learn the rules of the game.

21. Work to learn, not to earn

Getting out of the middle-class mental trap where everyone works to earn would take you to the world of the rich where people work to learn and hire others to do the earning bit. This is a mental shift and every business-owner must do this exercise if he does not want to be trapped forever in a 'job', even if it is for himself.

22. Give and you will receive

Whether it is love, respect, trust or just money, the more you give, the more you receive. This is a natural law. All really rich people are also very generous. But it is not only money that you should give. Your children need a lot of your time, attention and interest. Your spouse needs the same. Your employees would need your genuine care and interest in their careers and personal growth. By giving them this you will receive ten-folds in return.

23. Cultivate your mind

Your mind is your most valuable personal asset. By cultivating your mind you will ensure that all that we have discussed earlier and the many things that we have not discussed (because they are not the subject of this book) become a part of your growth. The mind remains active only if you use it. The human mind is capable of everything and its limits have never been tested. Use your mind by cultivating it.

24. Don't be afraid to seek answers

Answers are a dime a dozen, it is the right questions that are difficult to find. Most people are afraid to ask questions either because they are afraid to 'expose their ignorance' or because they believe they know everything. It is the questing mind that discovers new pathways, it is the curious mind that finds hidden treasures and it is this attitude that breaks open barriers to knowledge and wonder. We live in the Information Age. Use it to your advantage. The man who has access to information is the one who wins.

25. The longest journey begins with a single step

After all's said and done, our journey and

adventure ahead await your decision. To do or not to do, *that* is the question. Until you take that first step, your adventurous journey cannot begin. Once you take the first few steps, the next ones will become easier. Along the way, you will discover the strength and stamina to take you along further and you will also find the motivation to go on ahead. With each step of the journey, you will find some challenges and some rewards. And each step you take will take you closer to your ultimate goal of happiness.